# PRISONERS OF REVOLUTION

*a political novel*



Amar Mudi

olive turtle

NIYOGI BOOKS

Published by
**NIYOGI BOOKS**
Block D, Building No. 77,
Okhla Industrial Area, Phase-I,
New Delhi-110 020, INDIA
Tel: 91-11-26816301, 26818960
Email: niyogibooks@gmail.com
Website: www.niyogibooksindia.com



Editor: Arunima Ghosh
Cover design: Misha Oberoi
Inside layout: Shraboni Roy

ISBN: 978-93-89136-17-3
Publication: 2019



Printed at: Niyogi Offset Pvt. Ltd., New Delhi, India

*'In politics, we will be recognizing the principle of one man one vote and one vote one value. In our social and economic life, we shall, by reason of our social and economic structure, continue to deny the principle of one man one value. How long shall we continue to live this life of contradictions? How long shall we continue to deny equality in our social and economic life? If we continue to deny it for long, we will do so only by putting our political democracy in peril. We must remove this contradiction at the earliest possible moment or else those who suffer from inequality will blow up the structure of political democracy, which this assembly has so laboriously built up.'*

**Babasaheb Dr B.R. Ambedkar**

# Prologue

Chilka! It is very difficult to answer your questions: What went wrong? Why were so many lives lost? How could the dream of a revolution to change the social order be so brutally extinguished?

It was the mid-sixties when we heard the slogan for the first time: 'Workers of the world, unite!' For the first time someone told us about our right to own a piece of land, right to earn decent wages for the hard work we put in, and the battle we have to fight to achieve these goals.

We rallied behind the party holding aloft the red flag. The party recorded a massive win and formed a coalition government. Then we came to know about many shades of the red flag: blood red, pinkish red, etc. The dream was short-lived; the coalition didn't last. We were told that revolution comes through the barrel of a gun. We picked up the gun, waged war against unknown enemies, sometimes a big farmer, a police constable, or even a suspected neighbour. Some of us died heroic deaths, some rotted in jail, and some became untouchables in the society. Spring Thunder* lost its steam prematurely.

You asked me a question Chilka, 'Why did you people join the battle against the mighty state? Have you read Marx, Lenin, and Mao? Do you know, exactly, what are you fighting for?'

I have no clear answer. Will you accept, if I tell you that we are fighting for protecting Mother Earth from the greedy, who denude her by wiping out the green cover, emptying out her treasures, hidden deep inside, and mercilessly killing the dumb denizens of the serene abode? This is the continuation of a battle we have been fighting for ages. Who would know better than us what it means to live the life of a nomad after being driven out from one settlement to another for generations? When someone invites us to fight for changing the social order, we join them with the belief that tomorrow will be ours.

When I look back on those tumultuous years, I feel that the massive uprising in Bengal could not have happened out of the blue. It was the culmination of resistance to exploitation, by thousands of unknown heroes in the nondescript villages of Kerala, Tamil Nadu, Andhra, Odissa, Bihar, and other states; struggle against the mighty; and mobilization of the oppressed going on for so many past years. What happened on 24 May 1967 in Naxalbari and spread like wildfire had its genesis in Lalgonda, Kakdwip, Srikkulam, and other places.

---

* The May 1967 incident in the Naxalbari district of West Bengal, India, was called a 'spring thunder' in the article 'Spring Thunder Over India', first published in *People's Daily,* organ of the Central Committee of the Communist Party of China on 5 July 1967. The first line read as: 'A peal of spring thunder has crashed over the land of India....'

The only surprise, the unknown factor, in it was that, of all places, the volcano erupted in a village in North Bengal, the most backward region of the state, instead of any other from among the so-called politically conscious districts around Kolkata. One arrow shot in a moment of panic killed a police sub-inspector and all hell broke loose. Waves and waves of bullets showered upon unsuspecting people to quell the so-called uprising, but they stood their ground, and continued their fight. The mortal terror among the landlords was visible for the first time, when thousands of peasants marched ahead, waving the red flag across the paddy fields of Terai. Naxalbari became synonymous with the new found resurgence of the 'have-nots'.

Students in elite colleges and universities in Kolkata had read the stories of revolution in Russia and China, about the bloody battles of Petrograd and Yenan. They suddenly discovered that there was revolution in the air of their own country. They fanned out to villages and urban slums to mobilize the peasants and workers. They firmly believed that revolution comes out from the barrel of a gun—out of the pipe guns and handmade bombs, produced in scores in the lanes and the bylanes of Kolkata. They were told—'Eliminate the enemies of revolution! Create a Naxalbari of your own!'

What happened then, Chilka?

Suddenly, guns and bombs became more potent than human beings. Pitched battles were fought on the streets of the cities between the state and the cadres of the mainstream political parties on one hand, and the young brigade of revolutionaries on the other: between trained forces and a handful of starved men and women in the villages and jungles. It was an unequal battle.

The irony was that the momentum could not be sustained despite so much enthusiasm. A disconnect between the idealist young brigade and people around them became apparent very soon. Heads of statues of Bengali icons were rolled down, school and college libraries were torched, streets and lanes became killing fields, and all this happened in the name of class struggle. A mortal fear gripped the villages, towns, and cities alike. Streets became empty as soon as a single bomb exploded or a procession was lathi charged, tear-gassed, or fired upon. Coolies, thela walas and office going babus ran for their lives because they didn't believe that it was their fight. Their first and foremost concern was to save their own lives and the lives of their near and dear ones. Everything else came second to that: religion, country, belief, integrity, and right and wrong.

The inevitable happened after the empire struck back. After the initial resistance, it was a fratricidal war. A generation having the fire of revolution in their belly was either wiped out or incarcerated in prison for the better part of their lives. A section of lumpen elements took over the streets in the guise of workers of one political party or the other. The country went back into stupor for years to come.

# The Bhadraloks of Babulpur

I clearly remember the winter of 1966. It was ominous in the beginning. In the middle of November, people observed an aura around the moon on the full moon night. The elders of the village, called *murubbis*, recited a couplet from *Khanar Bachan* (*Khana*'s Words), by the legendary oracle Khana (pronounced as 'Khawna'):

When the moon is on its throne
Surrounded by his ministers
Tighten your girdle; Oh Farmers!
Protect the grains well at home.

Everyone knew that Khana's prophecies could not go wrong. To prove her *bachan* true, the very next afternoon, dark clouds suddenly appeared in the north-east sky. One shower at this point would ruin the semi-ripe paddy grains, which still required a fortnight of sunshine to mature for harvest. Even a mild thunderstorm would break the stems in the middle and the entire crop would turn into dead straw and husk without any grain inside.

My grandfather, Santosh Pradhan, was pacing along the verandah since he had looked at the sky and seen the cloud. The long verandah of our house was adorned with framed lithographs of numerous gods and goddesses: Shiva, Vishnu, Kali, and Laxmi co-existing peacefully. Bhupal Master, the caretaker cum accountant cum manager of the Pradhan house shouldered the responsibility of periodically wiping out the dust from the glass of the lithographs and also from the Anglo-Swiss wall clock hanging on the wall. He was not allowed to wind the clock. Santosh babu trusted only Naren, his eldest son, for this job.

Santosh Pradhan was the mukhiya of the village. He held his *durbaar* for the outsiders sitting on the only chair kept in the verandah. He always carried a handheld hookah of his own. Two wooden planks were earmarked for two categories of visitors, and two hookahs for two different classes of people on each side of the chair. Adivasis and lower caste Hindus lighted up the *kalke* or the mouthpiece, puffing it with all their might, before placing it on the hookah and handing it over to the babus.

Grandfather used to have his lunch sharp at twelve, sleep for an hour or two, and then prepare for himself a glass full of tea boiled in pure milk. After leisurely sipping the tea with two spoonful of *chyavanprash*, he used to go out to the verandah for taking stock of the day's work.

That afternoon, as soon as he came out, looked at the sky, and saw the cloud, creases appeared on his forehead. He had also seen the moon last night, the patch of dark cloud in the north-western sky and also a thin layer of cloud over the sun, which made it look like a well-polished brass plate. He immediately turned towards the first floor window and shouted,

'Naren! Naren!'

My father, who was having a post-lunch nap, appeared after a few minutes. His puffy eyes were proof enough of the deep slumber he was enjoying. He stood before his father like a guilty student awaiting punishment. Grandfather sat on his chair and took a deep drag of the hookah.

'Naren, this is not the time to sleep,' he said sternly.

This was followed by a list of instructions.

'Ask Dharma to refurbish the bullock carts and take the sickles to the blacksmith for sharpening. Indra, the lord of rain, and Ma Laxmi, the goddess of prosperity, seem to be angry upon us this year. Before the rain comes, we have to get the crop out of the field and stack it in our courtyard. Check the list of this year's borrowers. They must report for harvesting the paddy from the beginning, or else they should not expect any advance next season.'

Agor village was a few hundred metres from our house, mainly inhabited by Santhals. The workforce of our family came mainly from that village. A relationship developed between us and the Adivasis of this village because of the long association, and in some situations it went beyond that of the landlord and the labourer.

After sunset I accompanied Father. That evening when we entered the village, it was almost dark. Adivasi villages hide their scars of poverty and hunger under the dark veil of the night. It becomes very pleasant then. Mats are spread in the courtyards. Men and women sit together with a pot of *handiya* and talk about the day. A bowl is passed on till the stock lasts. The potent brew wipes out the sufferings. They sing, pour their heart out in songs; tunes come out of the string and drums. When we, father and son, entered the hut of Salge Ram, the song they were singing stopped abruptly. The half empty bowl was left unattended. We two sat down on one mat and the rest jostled for space on the other. Father started the conversation with the weather forecast, 'Salge bhai, have you noticed the sky today? It seems that the rain is imminent. Baba asked me to talk to you people. You should be free for harvesting the crop in one go, starting from day after.'

Salge and others of the village remained silent. With one look at them, Father sensed something was amiss. He asked, 'Is there any problem, Salge? Tell me frankly.'

Salge cleared his throat twice, and halting in between, he said, 'Naren bhai, as soon as we saw the red clouds in the west, we knew that Santosh babu would summon us soon. But... the party has called for a labour boycott for increase in wages. Hari bhai held a meeting in our *para* yesterday and we promised to support the boycott call.'

Father was visibly stunned. He cajoled them referring to the long relationship that the landowners and labourers/sharecroppers shared, threatened them about the dadan (the advance to tide over the lean period), and abused the leaders who poisoned their minds. They remained silent throughout. At last, Father realized the futility of further discussion, and we got up amidst complete silence.

A few rich farmers were informed that very night. They came down to our house at midnight to discuss their strategy. Rakhal babu strongly advocated a tough stand: 'We have to fight out this unreasonable demand. These illiterate savages should be taught a lesson. The assembly election will be held just after a few months. A soft stance at this juncture will only strengthen the communists. Let us see how long they survive without wages.'

Prankrishno declared his strategy: 'I anticipated this. I have already finalized a deal with the agent in Odissa. He will bring 20 labourers from Amarda for me. I have to pay them both in cash and kind, but still it will be a better bargain. Why can't the others do the same?'

Grandfather had another trick up his sleeve. 'Good. But you won't get them round the year. You have to depend on the local labourers sooner or later. My advice will be to offer a little higher wage and more rice to those who agree to work during the labour strike. That way, we can break their rank and be in a better position to bargain.' Finally, it was decided to wait and watch, even if that would damage the ripe paddy due to delay in harvesting.

However, Mother Nature proved to be benevolent that year. Farmers were spared with just a light rain and no storm. But both the sides had to be battle-ready. The Krishak Sabha decided to intensify their agitation for higher wages and declared total strike, much earlier than the previous years. Landlords also finalized their strategy and brought labourers from the border districts of Odissa. Local labourers resisted fiercely. Every morning the road along Babulpur witnessed a *michil* of the local labourers. Mostly Adivasi men and women, carrying fragments of torn red cloth tied around long sticks, marched to one stretch of a paddy field or the other to drive away the outsiders engaged by the landlords. Everyday there were incidents of violence in the paddy fields in the morning, which inevitably invited a jeep full of policemen by evening. They arrested a few people, tied them to one long rope, and dragged them to the police station as evidence of the action taken by them. The rumour was that Narayanpur Thana faced an acute shortage of handcuffs.

One incident, which shook the stupor out of Babulpur that winter, took place in Nuapada paddy field. Prankrishno owned a large tract of land there. He engaged labourers from Mayurbhanj, the neighbouring district in Odissa. And to stave off the agitating labourers, he also hired Heeru and his men to guard them. When Kartik and a few agitating labourers from Nuapada reached the field, they were severely beaten up. They fled the scene with tell-tale signs of injuries on their bodies.

Things went out of hand after the workers, who had assembled at Babulpur market, heard about it. They ran towards Nuapada in groups, shouting 'inquilab zindabad', waving the red flag. Heeru and his men shot a few arrows towards them to scare them away even when they were still at a considerable distance. The sloganeering stopped and the procession halted. But some of the younger Adivasi men, who carried their bows and arrows, took cover behind bushes and retaliated. One arrow of Subhas Soren found its mark and pierced deep into the thigh of one of Heeru's men. A roar went up into the sky, the long forgotten war cry. The mob charged like a victorious army, grabbed the goons as well as the migrant labourers, and thrashed them soundly.

When they found that they have been outnumbered, Prankrishno and his men ran away from the field. But they headed straight to

Narayanpur Thana after procuring medical reports for each of the injured from the government hospital, and lodged a report with the police. In the afternoon, a large contingent of police forces raided the Adivasi Para. Subhas was absconding. The police arrested two main Adivasi leaders of the party in Babulpur; Hari and Kanan and a few more young men were dragged out of the huts without any warrant. People present there protested, because they knew that these two men were not present in the Nuapada field at the time of the incident, but the police wielded lathi upon all those who questioned their arrest. They were dragged to the truck and packed off.

The incident acted as a spark and lighted the fire hidden so far within the minds of the working people of the entire village—both Adivasis and lower caste Bengalis, something that number of processions and meetings organized by the party in the past had failed to achieve. They were out on the road next morning with whatever arms they had: spears, axes, bows and arrows, or at least a well-oiled bamboo lathi. Next day a *michil* led by Paran, the angry young Adivasi, suddenly marched towards the house of Prankrishno and stood there in seize. The entire family fled in panic. A heavy police contingent saved the house from being burnt down. Hired labourers were in panic and they left Babulpur in the dark of the night. The frenzy dented the confidence of even the rich farmers. They remained inside their houses, guarded by the small workforce still loyal to their masters. The police made regular rounds in the village. Ripe paddy was drying up and wasting away. Eventually, all farmers, big and small, had to stoop down and accept the demand of the labourers to increase the wages partially, to save their crop.

Election for the state assembly was declared even before the paddy could be properly stored by the farmers. The recent victory of the labourers galvanized the image of the party. To cash in on that, the party managed to get Hari and Kanan out on bail. They were the two leaders, who had spearheaded the agitation of the peasants and labourers of Babulpur during the last few years, served two terms behind bars, and as a result, they became the face of the party to both Adivasi and Bengali poor peasants.

Time has its own way of shaping up the course of events. The absence of Hari, Kanan, and the other active leaders of the party created a vacuum, and nature abhors vacuum. By the time they returned, Babulpur witnessed the emergence of a new generation of Adivasis, who had only heard that their ancestors had migrated to this village from jungles and hills. They had no idea how those places were. They only knew that the people living in the huts on this side of Babui River spoke a language different from the people of the other side. The sole connection of the Adivasis with the people of the other side was that they worked in their fields as labourers. They knew nothing about the vast territory of the land which they called their *desh*, the land to which they belonged.

They worshipped the sky, the sun, the moon, the trees—the things that they witnessed when they opened their eyes for the first time on the bosom of this earth, and again, for the last time, when they close their eyes finally. These were real and beautiful as well. For ages, they composed songs, sang on festivals, and felt that the sky and the moon came down to the earth to sing and dance with them, to be a part of their happiness and sorrow. They could not decipher the words uttered before the idols they called gods and goddesses, neither did they understand why people stand there with folded hands and prostrate in fear of curses. Yet they were treated as outcasts and savages, as their ancestors came from an alien land and belonged to a different culture. The young Adivasis questioned the deference of the elders towards their masters, defied the customs as well as the segregation. They looked straight ahead and confronted the rich and the mighty, eye to eye, shrugging off the inferiority complex of the people of earlier generations, just because they lived a cluster away from the heart of Babulpur, on the other side of Babui River. They refused to accept that the village was an alien land for them. The young adivasis were determined not to leave Babulpur in the hands of the people who cared for the earth much less than them.

Subhas became the hero, as his arrows had inflicted the gravest damage upon the enemy so far, during an open confrontation. But he went underground and lost the respect reserved for a soldier who stands in the battlefield. Now, the mantle of leadership had passed on to Paran, who led the people to *gherao* (to ambush by surrounding) the house of Prankrishno.

# The Indoctrination

From the stories I have heard about the earth-shattering assembly election of 1967 in Babulpur, I am of the view that the real hero was Paran, the young leader of the Adivasis. Even after all these years, whenever anyone talked about that period, it was his bravery, his leadership quality that they remembered.

Paran was one of those few young Adivasis in Babulpur, who had been to school for a few years. He studied up to the sixth standard. He dropped out after his mother died and his father suffered a prolonged bout of fever. He had to work as a labourer to sustain his family for months. But even after his father recovered, he could not return to school. They had to repay a substantial amount of money they had borrowed from Nagen Mahajan for his mother's treatment. His father had to mortgage the only piece of land they owned on this earth. He worked hard with his father to repay the loan, and finally recovered the land.

However, the draught next year forced them, like the other poor people of Babulpur, to starve for days. As a last resort Paran joined the mob, which seized every *jotdar*'s ('jotdar' meaning a wealthy peasant) house, demanding rice and paddy as *dadan* to tide over the crisis.

One day, when a group of people from his *para* marched towards the house of Santosh Pradhan, he also joined them carrying a sack and hoping that they would also get a share of the paddy promised by Santosh babu. But the police and state government officers also arrived there at the same time to seize the surplus paddy stored by Santosh babu. He lost himself in the frenzy and fought a pitched battle with the police to send back the truck brought there to take the seized grains. It was an unequal battle. Though they fought tooth and nail, they failed to save the paddy they had produced even when they were starving. The police thrashed them black and blue, arrested Nuna along with the others present there, and registered cases of arson and looting after taking them into custody. He was among the fortunate ones, maybe because of his age, who escaped with a few blows of lathi here and there on his body. His father was slapped with minor offences, though the known faces like Hari, Kanan, and others, with past political records, faced serious charges.

Shortly after coming back from prison, his father died; some people said that he died due to prolonged illness, while others thought that it was hunger that felled him. Nobody knew how and when the young, obedient, and sincere Adivasi boy transformed into an angry, impatient adult.

Paran stopped working as a farm labourer thereafter. He decided to work as a labourer in Narayanpur town instead. He would go to the railway station early in the morning everyday and wait for his turn to unload the consignments that came by rail wagons for the local Marwari distributors of goods and ration. But his turn would come only one or two days in a week. On the other days, he used to try his luck in the rice mill, or come back empty-handed in the afternoon and roam around in one Adivasi Para or the other, spending whatever little money he had in his pocket on mahua or *handiya* (rice liquour), and sleep on empty stomach at night in his empty hut. His own people started avoiding Paran for his volatile temperament and his habit of picking up a fight at the slightest provocation. He asked uncomfortable questions in the party meetings whenever he was present. The speaker, for instance, said,

'Once our party comes to power, minimum wages will be double of what it is now, sharecroppers will get two-thirds of the produce, excess land, and land owned in fictitious names will be taken over by the government and distributed among the landless...'

Much to the annoyance of the speaker, Paran would ask, 'Do you want us to believe that once the government asks them, the *jotdars* will readily open their iron chest and give away money and land deeds? Have you ever seen a leopard change its spots?'

People present there murmured in support of him. For generations they had witnessed their land being snatched away; they were paid pittance for their labour. They knew that the tiger cannot wash away its stripes. But they could not tell this on the face of the leaders who were 'educated' and acquainted with the ways of the world. However, Paran did not believe them. He was there when the poor assembled before the house of Santosh babu, fought with the police for a little amount of paddy for their hungry families, believing the tall talks of these leaders. They were arrested, and for months they rot in jail. His father died, but no one lifted even a finger to help him. None of these leaders suffered. They didn't need to. But he knew in the heart of his heart that the other alternative before the people was to yoke themselves again to the plough of the rich farmers. There was no possibility of breaking free from the shackles of *dadan*, even if they went on repaying the loans for generations. Their dream of owning a piece of land during their lifetime would forever remain a dream.

Hari was released from jail on bail a few weeks before the election. Paran and some of his young friends came to Hari's hut that very evening. There was a big crowd of Adivasis and Bengalis. After sunset, most of the people left the place. Hari lied down on the mat woven with palm leaves. Joba came out hurriedly, put a *kantha* under his head, and sat beside him caressing his hair. Paran leaned over Hari and asked softly,

'Hari kaka, our netas are going to each Adivasi Para and telling people that if they win the election, it will be their own government. They will get better wages, get land after the surplus and *benami* lands of the big *jotdars* are confiscated, and the patta or land deeds will be in their name. But I don't believe these bhadraloks anymore.'

Hari ignored him and asked Joba for a biri instead. Joba frowned, and then with a smile, slapped him lovingly on his cheek. She was in the advanced stage of pregnancy and would take time to get up. Paran took one out of his pocket, lighted it, and offered it to Hari. Hari took a deep drag and smiled.

'Paran, biri is the most precious thing in jail, in exchange of which, you can get whatever you want. And my dear fat wife doesn't allow me to smoke even one biri here in my own house.'

Paran remained silent for a while, perhaps to understand why Hari was avoiding his question. He swallowed his pride and said, 'Hari kaka, two-three outsiders are roaming around in the village with Subhas at night. They tell the people that all these promises are nothing but false. These leaders are making an all-out effort to grab power through election, by being part of multiple parties like the Congress, the Bangla Congress, the Adi Congress, and so on. There is not much of a difference among these parties, including the one which claims to be the Communist Party. They say that nothing can be achieved unless the peasants take up arms to fight the battle for their right to live a dignified life, become the owners of the land they teal, and claim their rightful share of grains. We are confused, Hari bhai. We don't get food, if we don't work. If we want to work, we have to accept the wages offered by the *jotdars*. How do we fight, with what?'

Because of his prolonged illness and lung infection, Hari had been feeling drained after he came out of jail. He would be short of breath even on the slightest exertion. He had been badly hurt on his head in the scuffle at the time of his arrest a few months back. Later, while in jail, he suffered from tuberculosis. Even now, he was not in a position to speak for a few minutes at a stretch. But he got up and leaned on the bamboo pole, taking support of the bundle of cloth put behind his back for support by Joba. Hari took his time, and then said in a mellowed voice,

'Paran, God has given four strong legs to deer; they run away from their predators in whatever direction their legs take them, but eventually they fail to escape and fall prey to the cunning tiger. Look at the buffalo! The entire herd hits back, whenever any one of them is attacked. They strike back with whatever they have. They push back the predator, though they don't have fangs or claws, only because they are united in their fight. Our ancestors ran away from the aliens and feudal lords encroaching upon their territory time and again, leaving their huts and villages, lush green fields, and well preserved jungles which provided them honey and herbs. But we have inherited the legacy of a few of those brave Adivasis, who had taken matters into their hands and confronted the outside world head on. They refused to abide by the taboo of migrating to the alien land, the land of Dikus. Today, we are an integral part of the people of the mainland and no one can deny us our rights on the land and the harvest.

'It took two generations' sweat and blood to get a foothold in this territory of others. Many lives were lost due to hunger, disease, brutal killing... Today, these people are coming to the Adivasis because, we have become an integral part of this land, this country. They have realized our strength and they need our support. We cannot hide ourselves inside the cocoon anymore. We have to untangle the silk threads carefully, come out and take our people to the next level. Again, sacrifices will have to be made, lives will be lost, but we have to be firm in our resolve.

There will be temptations to settle the score with the *jotdars*—tooth for tooth, eye for an eye. But we have to take people along with us. Always! Everywhere! You have to read the minds of your own people and be sure whether they are ready to take up arms and fight. They will show you the path; give you the opportunity. I am clear about one thing: if *we* don't stand up now, the opportunity will be lost forever. Now, the choice is yours.'

Hari was finding it more and more difficult to sit erect. Putting his head on the makeshift pillow, he again stretched out on the mat and closed his eyes. Kanan waved at Paran and all those present there, signalling them to go out. After a few minutes he also joined them. They all stood there in silence for some time. Paran came closer to Kanan and asked almost in a whisper, 'Kanu kaka, has he gone mad? What is he saying? He has lost his head due to illness and imprisonment. Why is he asking all of us to fight, and in the same breath, telling us that we should go to people and ask them what we should do? Will anyone say that they want death, bloodbath, and all such nonsense?'

Kanu thumped his shoulder, and replied, 'He says many such things that I don't understand. He does many things we cannot even imagine. But one thing I know, he sees many things, which we don't see. His grandfather, Matu, once led the people out of the jungle and came to this land, defying the elders of the clan. He silently bore the curse hurled upon him. But he fought ferociously to secure a piece of land for the people and paid the price by sacrificing his life. Like him, Hari never asked you to follow him. He has given you a choice; follow him, or do whatever you think is best for you and your people. If you prove to be right, *he* will follow *you*.'

# The Carnival of Democracy

The transformation of a village that was inhabited by predominantly backward class people with little or no education, from conservative Congressism to leftist aggression within a span of few years, often amazed me. I tried to recreate the chronology of events to understand the puzzle.

Only about a week was left for the assembly election. Debendranath Das, one of the most respected freedom fighters of Midnapur district, was roped in by Congress to come to Narayanpur and speak at the public meeting after a long gap. He belonged to a rich family in Dantan, but in 1939, he left his family business, donned khadi, and joined Congress. He was in the forefront of the Quit India Movement and went to jail many times during the struggle against British rule. He was the MLA of Dantan for many years after independence. Lately, he had withdrawn himself from active politics due to old age, but people still remembered him as an honest political leader and a good orator. The people from the entire stretch, from Babulpur to the north of Babui River, went together to have a glimpse of him. In a frail voice, he addressed the people:

'An ominous red cloud is hovering in the horizon. Our district has the glorious history of defeating the red skins through non-violent *satyagraha*, but this red party is no different from them. They do not believe in non-violence. They want to launch a bloody revolution on this land of the Buddha and Mahatma Gandhi. Time has come again for forging unity among people, the rich and the poor, lower and upper castes, irrespective of religion, to ward off violence.'

There was an eerie silence in the village market the next day; big or small, the farmers gathered in small groups in the house of one or the other to discuss the implication of the forecast Deben babu had made. The signs were indeed ominous for the farmers dependent on labourers for cultivation. Khet Majdur strike, unheard of even five years back, was now a routine every season, forcing the big farmers to dole out higher and higher wages; the demand of the sharecroppers for land rights was getting shriller by the day. The time was not far when the big farmers would have to give away their ancestral lands to the Adivasis and untouchables, who had already got their share out of the lands donated during the Bhoodan Movement*. The unanimous view was that it was time for the middle class and rich farmers to unite, and take some drastic action to finish the troublemakers once for all, before they grew larger in numbers and got out of control.

The meeting of the Communist Party to counter the rally addressed by Deben babu was scheduled a few days later. Everybody in

* The Bhoodan Movement or Land Gift Movement, was a voluntary land reform movement in India, started by Acharya Vinoba Bhave in 1951. Their mission was to persuade wealthy landowners to voluntarily give a percentage of their land to the landless people. However, this land could not be sold. In effect, landless labourers were given small plots of land on which they could settle, as well as grow some of their own food. The movement, though independent of the government, had the support of Congress.

Babulpur was cock-sure about the futility of it and the poor response it will get, but not Paran. He exhorted everyone to join the rally. Fifty-odd people gathered by noon. Paran led the small group hurling the only flag with the hammer-sickle-star sign available in the village. Others tied pieces of red cloth to bamboo poles and waved those with all their might, shouted at the top of their lungs, and marched towards Narayanpur for the meeting.

Suddenly, they saw another procession of Congress supporters coming from the opposite direction. Balai babu's son, Prankrishno, known as a bully and womanizer, was in the forefront. He must have exhorted other young men from the middle class and rich families with people loyal to them to join the procession. He also engaged Heeru and his men to be with them to help if required. Somehow, it became a decent gathering for a final show of strength, a week before the election.

Two processions marched from two opposite directions on the narrow road and came face to face just outside Babulpur in the north. Rakhal Singh, the carpenter, whispered in the ears of Paran, 'Bhai, let us take a detour. I know they are going to create some trouble.' Paran looked at him for a few seconds and said, 'If you want, you can go. I will not. Ask the others and take those with you who want to leave.'

Rakhal kept quiet and slipped to the back, but didn't leave. The march slowed down. Eventually, when the two groups confronted, the small group of men and women with the red flag left the road to pave way for the other procession to proceed, but Paran stood his ground with the party flag on his shoulder. Had it been any other party leader from Midnapur, or even Narayanpur, Prankrishno would have behaved in a different way; but an Adivasi labourer challenging the might of the farmers from whom they have begged for work and rice from time immemorial in order to survive, was something beyond the limit of his tolerance. Prankrishno shouted, 'Paran, get out of the way!'

Paran looked straight at him and said, 'Why? We are going our way; there is enough space for you to pass.'

By that time, they had come even closer, and almost everybody behind Paran had left the road. The lone man obstructing the path of the procession looked rather comical. If ignored, it would be his victory. Prankrishno had no other option, but to push him away from the road. He was not ready for retaliation from Paran. He staggered. The moment he regained himself, he shouted, 'Beat these bastards up! Pulp their bones!'

Heeru and his men pounced upon the motley group of men, women, and children, wielding their lathi mercilessly. The hapless people ran helter-skelter after putting up mild resistance, leaving Paran, who was by then surrounded by Heeru and some of his men. It became obvious that their prime target was Paran, when the rest of the group abandoned their chase, turned back, and encircled him. Seeing this, those who were running away stopped where they were. Few of them even started walking back.

That was the moment when Paran remembered Hari's words: 'If we don't stand up now, we will lose everything we have gained so far.'

Like a lone dog surrounded by foes in an alien territory, he coiled up to protect his head and shoulders from the lathi blows, and succeeded in taking most of the them on his hands and back. Despite being cornered, he managed to catch hold of and snatch a well oiled bamboo pole from the man holding it. Paran pounced upon the weakest person among the attackers and dealt a severe blow. The man sagged. Paran leaped over his body and joined his people who were standing a few metres away. Finding him back among them, they regrouped, picked up bamboo poles from the fences, stones and bricks, or whatever they could lay their hands on, and attacked the men accompanying Prankrishno, shouting the war cry long forgotten, after the egress of their ancestors from the Lulung forest, their homeland. The men on the other side panicked and tried to shield their young masters scurrying for cover. Within a few seconds, they fled from the scene taking different routes, leaving the small group of party workers with mangled flags and bruised bodies, but in high spirits to carry on the procession.

The incident had wide repercussions. Paran and his comrades were taken up on the stage at Narayanpur. Speaker after speaker spew fire against the rival party, showing the wounds and bruises on their bodies. Babulpur was agog with rumours of armed Adivasis coming down to take revenge. Though there was no legitimate basis of the rumour, the division among the voters in the community became obvious. Leaders of both parties, the Congress and the Communist, planned only cluster meetings in the night, instead of rallies and open show of strength. The party made arrangements for Hari to address the Adivasis in Babulpur as well as in the nearby villages, for the compelling reason that he was an Adivasi himself, and everyone knew that his words were taken as the advice of the leader of the local Adivasis, the descendant of Matu.

In one such meeting, Paran met Hari, who now looked his usual self. Paran could not believe what he heard. Instead of talking about the election and the party, Hari talked about Sidhu and Kanu, two

Adivasi brothers, who led the revolt against the British; how they fought valiantly for an independent identity of Adivasis, how they were killed by the British, and why they are still remembered by both Adivasis and non-Adivasis. People listening to him were mesmerized; some touched his feet, elders hugged him and blessed him. Paran realized that the votes of this pocket were secured without even asking for it.

After the meeting, they were invited for rice liquor and pork. In a lighter vein, Hari narrated his plight. Hadam, Hari's father, had offered a domestic fowl at the altar of Bonga, consecrated under the Banyan tree that was said to have sprung up magically in the premises of Sanatan Manjhi. The fowl had been reared by Joba, his wife. So she did not join Hadam; she could not have tolerated the ritual of beheading the bird so affectionately reared by her. Instead, she plucked a basket full of *sushni* leaves despite her swollen abdomen and cooked them with fenugreek seeds in the traditional way for Hari.

'So, I consumed the rooster curry with *handiya*, mixing it with fried *sushni* leaves, with a straight face, and both *baap* (father) and *bibi* (wife) were happy.'

As soon as they were alone, Hari patted Paran on his back and said, 'Well done, my boy! But henceforth, be careful. You have pricked the bee-hive. Be ready for the retaliation! They will try to provoke you on and off. Storm hits the big trees again and again till they are felled.'

Paran knew that. He witnessed the hostility in the eyes of the landlords and their henchmen whenever they met on the other side of Babui River; but he had other pressing issues to settle. He asked Hari, 'I have seen the voters' list of our gram panchayat. Many of the Adivasi voters' names are missing. We are outnumbered badly. I think the picture is same everywhere. We will be much less in number compared to them, if we cannot bring the Dhopas (washermen), Napits (barbers), Bagdis (indigenous people with Dravidian links), and the poor lower caste Bengalis together with Mahatos and Adivasis on our side. What do we do now?'

Hari was surprised when he heard Paran's strategy and realized that the understanding of ground reality of this young man with little or no exposure to politics was much better than the leaders'. During the last few years, he had learnt from his own experience that whenever there was any agitation in Babulpur, there was a division between the two communities: the tribals, and the poorer sections of Bengalis, even if the cause was common for them. He talked extensively to people to understand the reason. At last, he came to the conclusion that the Communist Party in Babulpur was largely confined to the Adivasis, because despite the exploitation the poor Hindus faced in the name of religion, despite the hunger they faced day in and day out, and despite the penury of almost everyone in their community, they refused to acknowledge any cause commonly with the Adivasis.

The lower caste Hindus and Harijans are ostracized by upper caste Bengali Hindus, yet they identify with the Bengali Hindu community, because caste-based division of society happened thousands of years back, and that is where they thought they traditionally belonged. They assumed that their current suffering was a result of the deeds of their past lives and that their sacrifices in this life would elevate them to a higher caste in the next. They hesitated to stand alongside the Adivasis even after a generation-long period of cohabitation, for they thought of the Adivasis as aliens and savages who spoke a different language and followed different religions and traditions. The barbers, washermen, or even the lowliest scavengers in the social order of the Hindu community thought themselves to be superior to the Adivasis, and refused to walk alongside them in the procession or sit with them during village meetings.

Hari thumped his shoulder and said, 'You are right. Manik babu and Sudhangshu babu approached them, but didn't get any response. They are afraid that if they join us, the Adivasis, they will be excommunicated from the Hindu *samaj*, which they believe they are part of. Why don't you talk to them? They don't suffer any less than us; they are equally exploited by the *jotdars*. Wearing shirts and dhotis discarded by their rich masters, they run errands for them on empty stomach.

Get Kartik, the barber, from Nuapada, to accompany you. He is also a lower caste Hindu, but one of the best party workers. Tell them that the party is fighting for the rights of the labourers, the sharecroppers, and the poor among both Hindus and Adivasis. The party has nothing to do with your religion or mine. Even after casting your vote to please the landlords for the last 20 years, where do you stand today? Don't be afraid! Nothing worse can happen to you.'

Paran worked upon the idea given by Hari and planned his strategy. He remembered that he had developed some kind of friendship with Bhola, the son of Khudi Sheet, from the Dhopa or washermen community of Babulpur. They were in the same class in school and both dropped out almost at the same time. One Thursday evening, he kept Bhola under watch from the weekly market and followed him when he returned home. After the evening grew a bit darker, he wrapped a cloth over his head and dropped in at Bhola's house. Bhola was scared.

'Paran, how come you are here? If somebody recognizes you here, all hell will break loose. Prankrishno babu has sworn by the name of Goddess Durga to teach you a lesson. They will kill you as well as me.'

Paran laughed and said, 'I know. But Bhola, neither I, nor you will be able to live long otherwise also. My father died due to hunger. Your father died, because you could not give him a drop of medicine. Why can't we try one last time to break the shackle of poverty and see if we can do something to change our plight for better, and then die?'

Bhola remained silent. A few seconds later, Basanti, his wife, broke the silence from behind the door. She said in hushed voice, 'Why don't you tell him how you are running your family? He won't... Let me tell you: last year during the draught, he mortgaged his land, and then pawned my ornaments, and now he has pawned me. Otherwise, we would have died of hunger, or committed suicide.'

Paran was taken aback. So long, he had thought that the Adivasis were the most exploited. He didn't believe Hari fully, when he told him about the helpless condition of the poor lower caste Bengalis. After he came to know of the situation of Bhola and Basanti, he could not control himself. For the first time, he addressed a Hindu woman as if she was one from her own community.

'Basanti, mark my words! Our time has come. Throughout the country, the poor and downtrodden are now united in fighting for their rights. It is for us to join them and strengthen their hands, or remain slaves for the rest of our lives. This vote is an opportunity for us to defeat them and bring communists to power. The party will support the people's struggle. But I shall not force Bhola. He should think it over and then decide.'

When he was about to come out, he heard Basanti's voice and looked back. She came out in the open. Her head cover slipped down. Paran could see that her face was livid with rage. She directly addressed him and said, 'I know that the other day you had been brutally beaten by that bastard Prankrishno. But you fought your way out and gave them a befitting reply. This is the first time someone has stood his ground against him.'

Pointing a finger towards Bhola, she continued, 'What he does is his business. I shall vote for the *kaste-haturi-tara* (sickle-hammer-star); and also ask other women to do that.'

Paran's throat choked with emotion. He almost ran towards Budha's liquor shop. Kanan was there with three-four other comrades. Paran joined them, and told Kanan about the development. All of them celebrated with a bottle of mahua. Kanan told them to follow it up with visits to the pockets of lower caste Bengalis silently and keep it secret. An invisible power had pulled Paran towards Bhola's house, which he could not resist.

The primary school of Babulpur was converted into the polling booth for the village. Well-dressed womenfolk of rich and middle class Bengalis thronged the booth since morning with children in tow. The whole atmosphere resembled a village fair. The makeshift stalls of Govinda selling *papad* and Haru selling *paan* witnessed brisk sales. Prankrishno and other Congress workers put up their covered kiosks just outside the statutory limit of the booth. On the opposite side of the road, Paran and his comrades placed only a cot they could arrange, and placed it under the shade of a babul tree that barely gave them protection from the scorching sun. Both sides were busy giving last minute instructions to their supporters on how to put the stamp on the twin ox, the election symbol of the Congress, or the sickle-hammer-star of the Communist Party of India, Marxists (CPIM).

The first sign of tension surfaced when Basanti and few other women of their village reached the polling booth. Prankrishno and his companions immediately surrounded them with dummy ballot papers, and shouted, pointing out to their symbol: 'Here is the twin bull. Put the stamp on it. Come, take your voter's slip.' Basanti flatly refused to even look at them and proceeded towards the opposite camp. The other women followed her. Paran, the only literate man, was sitting on a cot on the opposite side of the road. He wrote the part number and serial number of each of them from the voters' list on separate slips and handed those over to the group led by Basanti.

Prankrishno was dumbfounded for a moment at the audacity of these lower caste women, who had never dared to defy the orders of the village head in the past. He and some of his friends visited their huts regularly, for which they paid by cash and also handed out favours to their families. This was the tradition of the village. His humiliation by none other than Basanti, in particular, made him furious. It became uncontrollable, when he saw Basanti talking to Paran and laughing on and off. He swore at the women first, and then at Paran. Sensing his mood, other workers started hurling choicest abuses at these women, as they returned from the polling booth, along with indecent gestures, 'These harlots seek new pastures every night. Now, they have crossed over to the side of *junglees* (uncivilized). Arré, we are still capable of satisfying you.'

Bhola had been following Basanti and the other women of his *para*, anticipating some trouble. He was standing silently a few yards away from the polling booth with some of his neighbours, when all this happened. He could not tolerate the abuses anymore and howled at them, 'Shut up! Will you? Or I will kill you bastards!' Everyone looked back. Bhola took two steps towards Prankrishno and said, 'Do you think you will get our votes even after publicly insulting our women? She has done the right thing. You can never change...'

Before he could finish, Prankrishno lunged upon him and hit him with his fists. Bhola also retaliated. People from both sides intervened. The police had been keeping a watch. As soon as the policemen were seen coming towards them, both the groups retreated. Bhola limped towards the polling booth along with others, as if he wanted to settle the score in the ballot box, then and there. Prankrishno looked around. His eyes got riveted on a bare bodied man standing across the road and smiling. It was Paran. He again swore to himself to take revenge on this man, the root cause of all the trouble, at the first opportunity.

Harijan Para voted to the last man in the hammer-sickle-star symbol of the party. Their candidate won the Narayanpur assembly seat with thumping majority. United Front cobbled up majority in the assembly. There were celebrations all around the state and Babulpur did not lag behind.

# Celebration of Birth and Death

My father, Hari, believed that I was the reason for the untimely death of my mother on the day the party celebrated its victory in the assembly election. So did my grandfather, Hadam, but with a difference. Hadam swore upon everything he valued in this world and asserted that it was the curse of Badam Pahar, the abode of supreme power, which Joba took upon herself and sacrificed her life to save Hari and his son. Hadam believed that I, the son of Hari and Joba, was destined to accomplish the unfinished task of his great grandfather, Matu.

Matu led a small group of his friends and followers out of the jungles, defying the age-old tradition of the Adivasis to confine themselves in the hills, away from the gaze of the outside world to keep their age-old customs and traditions alive. Matu believed that the Adivasis needed to come out of thousands of years of isolation to survive in the changed environment of the world they lived in. Just before they left their village, the Manjhi Chief of the seven villages pronounced the curse in the name of their protector,

Badam Pahar, that a cruel, lonely death would await Matu and his family, wherever they would live.

The curse haunted the Adivasis of Babulpur every time death visited the family of Matu. On one chilly winter night, Matu was killed in the paddy fields, trying to protect the paddy of his master. His wife, Barak, died unattended, vomiting blood, leaving their son, Hadam, a destitute. Rajo, the elder son of Hadam, embraced Christianity and committed suicide after he was excommunicated from the family and the village for that.

A few elderly women of the Adivasi Para, with considerable experience about abortion and child birth, refused to believe Hadam and rubbished the bullshit about the 'curse' he was spreading. For them, the idea of reincarnation of Matu and such other accounts were creations of the imagination of the old man, who had lost his head due to drinking liquor day and night, so common among the people of his age.

Karma Budhi asked point-blank, 'Didn't you notice how Joba's face glowed like the progressing moon during each month of pregnancy, her breasts and abdomen swelled like jackfruit, but her hands and feet dried up like the pumpkin creeper?' Those were sure signs of the evil forces overpowering her with the avowed objective of turning her into a witch. She must have resisted, because she was asked to make a sacrifice of someone dear to her, which she turned down. Ultimately, she had to pay the price with her own life. Otherwise, why a strong and stout woman like Joba, who had already delivered a healthy girl child at a much younger age and had withstood the tantrums of a bull like Hari for so many years, could not eject a baby, more or less like a mole, from her womb? Their suspicion pointed towards the obvious: Asha, the widow. She had defied every single custom of the community, she became the main attraction in her father's—Budha's *handiya* den, ever since she came back as a widow; people loved to drink out of her hands. But not even once had she approached Pema Dhai or any other midwife in so many years to abort. She was the closest friend of Joba and also very close to Hari. Who was going to prevent her from eying at a readymade family once Joba is out of the scene?

My father, Hari, refused to even look at me for the first few days. He was angry, because he believed that Joba had betrayed his trust. She had assured Hari that nothing would happen to her. Hugging him tightly, she had whispered in his ears,

'Go ahead, Haria! Celebrate the day! The bitter fight of three generations of Adivasis has borne fruit. You have given your all for the party, you have mobilized the Adivasis for the party and have won them the election. Now, they have realized that they are capable of becoming the kingmaker in every election because their votes matter. You should be among your people, who have trusted you and have stood by you solidly. Don't worry! Nothing will happen to me.'

After Hari left with my sister, Sarasati, we—my mother and I, her yet to be born son—were alone in the hut for a considerable period of time. Just when the crowd chanted 'Inquilab Jindabad' for the the first time, Joba clutched her abdomen as if someone had stabbed her with a knife. She cried out in agony. Hadam woke up from slumber and rushed inside the hut. Seeing her condition he thought it wise to call Pema, the midwife, who lived in the southern end of the village.

'Baahu, get a grip on yourself. Sip some water from time to time from this pot. I am going to get Pema here as soon as possible.'

Joba perhaps had had a premonition that something ominous was going to happen to her or her child, but she didn't have the heart to hold Hari back. Had Hari been by her side, she might have been able to endure the excruciating pain of the troubled delivery, but she could not deprive her 'Haria' of his legitimate place at the time of victory celebration. Who knew better than her that he could not survive without his people and his party? Or perhaps, Hadam was right; the 'curse' did not come down upon Joba, she took it upon herself. Hari was sent away to take up the mantle of leadership of his clan for years to come. His son came out tearing the womb of his mother, to inflict several such bloodbaths upon the dead and rotten society, to bring it back to life. Hari would have sacrificed the unborn child to save Joba. Indeed the 'curse' had its strange way of goading each one to his or her destiny in different ways.

I carried inside me the memory of those painful hours etched permanently in my mind. Beneath this layer, lie many more such layers of memories of countless moments of death and devastation in the life of an Adivasi and his/her community. Each of these memories are reminders that the journey from the lap of Mother Nature for thousands of years could not have happened without a viable philosophy to sustain the onslaught. Like many other animals and tribes around the world, they would have been extinct by now from the face of the earth.

We shared the bounties of Mother Earth with insects, reptiles and animals, and thought that there is enough of it for all of us to live happily. We sang songs, danced, made merry with whatever we had. But we were ignorant about the greed of a few people belonging to our own species, who entered into our territory from the horizon, claimed to be a superior race and more powerful, and tried to enslave us to make their own lives comfortable. They called us *asur*, *naga*, monkey, and so on, and said that our place is in the nether world. We resisted. Thousands were killed, thousands more were captured alive, chained, and taken away as slaves. The rest took refuge in deeper jungles, in far away hills to start life afresh. But now we have reached a stage, when our back is against the wall. We have to break open a passage if we want to survive. Who lives and who dies in this process mattered very little for my mother, Joba, as well as for me.

Everything was alright till 2 o'clock. The moment the large stick struck the *dhamsa*, specially requisitioned for the victory march, signalling the procession to move, the sound reverberated through the entire village. It must have taken a fraction of a second more, but the vibration reached the Adivasi Para nonetheless, and from there, it entered the hut of Hari and resonated inside Joba. Hadam recounted later, 'That very moment Joba cried out for the first time, "Oi *gidra*! Don't kick me like that."'

From then onwards, the spasm and pain increased rapidly. Within an hour it became so intense that Joba told her father-in-law, 'Baap, go to Pema Dhai and ask her to come immediately.' She was consulting Pema, the midwife, off and on. Hadam thought that it would be better to rush even though Joba would have to be left alone.

When she realized that she was alone, a fear gripped her. She applied every household medicine she was familiar with to ease the pain: applied linseed oil, rubbed it with cold water, and so on, but nothing worked. She realized that the demon inside was clawing its way out by tearing her abdomen. She swore in the name of Jaher Bir, cried out to Bonga for help, but all in vain. Anger and frustration erased all high sounding words like 'love' and 'sacrifice' for her baby, her husband, her daughter, the whole world. She wanted to get rid of the lump in her abdomen that was killing her. Gasping for breath, she cursed the unborn—

'Come out you swine! Come out dead or alive! I don't care!

That drunkard, fornicating bull tore me apart every night, sowed the seed, and slipped away... Do me a favour, my child! Come out!'

I have carried you for all these days, have fed you the last drop of my blood. Is this what I get in return from you and your father? Spare me now! Let me live.

O Daramma Boi, have pity on me. Pull out the wolf out of my womb if you can, right now. It is tearing my flesh inside. It is a killer. It will kill many more, if it survives. For God's sake, come out! Let me live!'

Gradually, her voice mellowed down to a whisper. She lisped, but continued nonetheless.

'You demon! You are crushing me to death. Death! But remember, death is painful. Leaving your dear ones is painful. Leaving your dreams unfulfilled is painful. You will feel it. You must.'

My mother cried out in agony, till her last breath, in an effort to harness energy, squeezed her abdomen, burning the last ounce of her vitality to eject the puddle of flesh stuck in the orifice between her uterus and vagina. She succeeded, but the moment the choked infant came out to breathe in the open air, a gush of blood flooded the soil beneath; a vein or an artery must have snapped.

Hadam and Pema were the first to reach Joba. By the time they entered the hut, it was all over. She lay with eyes wide open and nails dug deep into her clenched fists. Pema said, 'This child was in a tearing hurry, as if he wanted to join the victory rally and shout *inquilab zindabad* alongside his father. He came out pushing the womb open. Poor Joba died due to excessive bleeding.' But I know, hadn't she succeeded in ejecting me from the passage for another few seconds, I wouldn't have lived to see this enchanting world.

That day signalled the end of one part of the quest that had begun many years back, when my great grandfather, Matu, left Lulung forest in search of a new world. He died before he could realize his dream of finding a place for himself and his people in the land they adopted, among the people of the plains. They only had a hut to live in, rice to eat, and the option to work as a farm labourer, but no land to sow seeds. After all the hard work they put together to produce plenty of grains and vegetables for others, they were treated as nothing but savages who had migrated from a distant land. Today, his grandson, Hari, succeeded in carving a place for them in the land of Dikus by becoming the deciding factor in the election. This election heralded a new don, not only for the Adivasis, for those lower caste people, who were glorified as Harijans, but were exploited for generations as much.

The news of Joba's death reached the people in the victory procession just before it was about to culminate in the school ground.

Someone informed Hari, 'Joba has given birth to a son.'

Hari smiled sheepishly and said, 'Bir Shukra came down on the right day.'

As he was proceeding to resume his place in the procession, the man whispered, 'Come with me, Hari. Joba is no more.'

Hari stood still for a few seconds, like a tree struck by lightning, shorn of branches, leaves, and flowers. His head tilted towards the sky, as if he was asking questions to that mysterious entity in heaven, 'Where have you gone? Where? Why? How can you?' He ran towards the Babui Bridge, which lay across the Adivasi Para, to his hut, where lifeless Joba lay.

It was that familiar scene when someone in the family dies. The dead body was sorrounded by mourning relatives and neighbours recounting the good and the bad deeds of the departed soul. The only difference here was the incessant shrill cry of the new born baby, hungry for succour, for the breast milk of its mother. Hari sat in one corner silently. Not even for once did he look at his just born baby, lying in the lap of Pema, covered in a bundle of cloth. He didn't look up at Hadam, who slumped over him, after he tried in vain to hug him. Someone from behind took him away from Hari.

The situation changed rapidly. Asha's yelling from quite a distance pierced the thin clay and bamboo wall of the hut. The people inside moved to make way for her, even before she entered with Sarasati in tow. She was discharging the responsibility given to her by Hari, when he had to move on to the front of the procession to get it started. She stood in silence for a few moments, and then threw herself upon Joba's cold body, crying: 'Joba, get up! Feed your baby! It has been crying since long… Look at your Haria! He will not survive the shock What will happen to Sarasati? Who will take care of this beautiful daughter of yours?' Sarasati had stopped crying since she had entered the hut with Asha. She was staring at her mother's motionless body with wide open eyes. Asha looked around, pulled her into a hug and they wept together.

Asha stopped all of a sudden. She got up, as if she had remembered something more important than crying over the dead. She turned back and moved closer to Hari. Kneeling down before him, she whispered, 'Get up! Sudhi Master and others will come any time now. Ask Kanan to make some arrangement for the cremation as soon as they can. It is already dark. I am taking the baby with me. I have to arrange a little goat milk to feed it; otherwise, it will not survive. Sarasati will also be with me. Don't worry.'

Hari didn't respond. She turned back, tidied up the blood soaked, worn out sari that Joba was wearing, and covered her body with a cleaner one. Everyone inside the hut had been following each of her movements. But they were in for a shock of their lifetime, when they saw her taking the baby, who had now started to cry hoarse in hunger, from Pema's lap, going to a corner, and clutching it to her breast. The baby went on rubbing its lips on her breast and searched for the nipple instinctively. Asha removed her blouse and sari from her left breast and offered the nipple to it. As the baby began suckling at the dry nipple, Asha shrieked. Nonetheless, the baby stopped crying to everyone's relief.

And that was the moment Sudhi Master entered the hut with his entourage. He sat down on the floor near Hari. His companions sat by his side. There was pin drop silence inside the hut. Sudhi Master cleared his throat, which everyone knew was the precursor of a long speech. He began with a sombre voice befitting the occasion.

'Comrade Hari, we are deeply pained at the sudden demise of your wife. She died on a great day, the day when our party assumed power in the state. Her sacrifice was for a noble cause. It will strengthen the party further.'

Asha got up, went closer to him, and said, 'Sudhi babu, Joba died at noon. Night has already set in. If we delay the last rites anymore, we will have to wait till the morning. We must proceed for her cremation immediately. We should not postpone it for tomorrow morning.'

Then it was Paran who shouted from the back of the people assembled there, 'Hari does not have money to buy the things required for the last rites. It is important to quickly arrange enough money for the cremation. If you can contribute something from the party fund, it is alright, or at least give something as a personal loan to me. I shall repay it within a few days.'

Sudhi babu fumbled, but he managed to keep his calm, and took out a few ten rupee notes from his bag. He came to the corner, where Hari sat like a stone figure. Hari did not respond to his overture. Sudhi babu ignored Asha and Paran, pushed the crumpled notes into the clenched fist of Hari, got up, and went out of the hut without uttering another word.

The elders decided to give Joba a decent cremation on the right bank of Babui River. After all, she had proved herself to be an ideal Adivasi *baahu* during her lifetime. Joba became an inseparable part of the Matu clan since the day Rajo, her first husband and the eldest son of Hadam, rubbed vermilion on her forehead in the Makar Sankranti fair. She refused to side with Rajo after he converted to Christianity. With a broken heart, Rajo committed suicide. Joba did not go back to her parents, nor tried to find another partner. She looked after her father-in-law and her daughter out of the meagre wages she earned. After his brother's death, Hari, the second son of Hadam, returned from Kolkata. How she persuaded Hari to stay back in the village, ignoring the lure of the city of Kolkata and got married to him, is still a mystery. Now, even when she died, she crowned herself with the glory of giving birth to a robust baby son to continue the lineage of Matu and Hadam.

Sanatan Manjhi proceeded in advance to prepare the pyre and perform the pre-cremation rituals for the dead. It took hardly a few minutes to cut down the neem tree in the courtyard after several hands wielded axe with all their might. There was an unprecedented gathering of Adivasi men and women on the banks of Babui. A large number of people came from other villages also, after the news reached through word of mouth of the people who had come to join the procession. Sanatan Manjhi placed five sal leaf plates on the ground adjacent to the pyre and offered rice, dal, vegetables, and black sesame, one for the last supper of the departed soul and four for the ancestors.

Hadam believed in what he had heard from the elders—that ancestors come down from their abode in heaven when someone from the family is about to join them. That they will come down for the most precious woman of their family was a certainty for him as well as everybody else. All those present there witnessed the bizarre incident that took place, when the pyre was lit. The smoke that bellowed out of the logs of the neem tree from Hadam's courtyard took the shape of Matu, Rajo, and other ancestors. Hadam went on shouting, 'Ha... Ha... Ha... Matu... Bap... Ha re... Rajo... Mai go....' Flames leapt up and consumed Joba's frail body. The smoke from the dying amber took the shape of Joba and the shadows disappeared altogether. Hari brought pots of water from the river and extinguished the flame. Sanatan reclaimed a few pieces of bones from the ashes still hot enough to scald the skin of his palm and handed over to Hari in a pot to be immersed later in the river, Damodar.

# Children get their Mother Back

Spring brings an end to the Ravi season after the crop is harvested. Kharif season starts in summer, leaving two months to the farmers to tighten their loin cloth. The boundaries of each plot of land is re-laid and strengthened to hold the rain water. Water is a very precious commodity in almost entire Bengal. The farmers of Babulpur also suffered due to scarcity of water, because there was no irrigation.

River Babui was like a small local cow that eats little and produces a litre or two of milk only for a few months. Babui came alive during the rainy season only. Whenever the mighty Subarnarekha broke the small barrier between the two, Babui washed away the huts and paddy fields till it pours down the water into Keleghai River, a few kilometres towards the east of Babulpur. The farmers solely depended on rain, the bounty of unpredictable nature, which often failed, and compelled people to starve for a year. A few skirmishes among the landowners were very common every year. But this year it escalated.

Harekrishna Konar, the Land Revenue Minister of the United Front government, who was the president of the Krishak Sabha till election, promised in meeting after meeting: 'Those, who till the land, shall be the owner of land!' The Adivasis, Bagdis, Mahatos, and Mahalis, who worked as labourers of the big farmers, knew who were the sharecroppers of which land. Believing his words, they demanded ownership of the lands for themselves after the Front came to power. It was free for all, till the owners went to court with all the documents they had prepared meticulously. The court intervened and upheld the ownership rights of the landlords and the government succumbed, leaving the poor peasants burnt from both ends.

The chief minister, elected by consensus, belonged to the Bangla Congress, an offshoot of the Congress of the old. He succeeded in keeping the mouths of his colleagues shut with the only ace he had: by threatening to resign and dislodge them from the throne. And it was a field day for the local officers and the police, who became the ultimate arbitrators between the haves and have-nots.

The volatile situation took its toll on my family. My father, Hari, was unanimously elected Secretary of the local Krishak Sabha, and got roasted in the political cauldron. He had no time to sleep, eat, or even take a proper bath due to the incessant call of distressed labourers, sharecroppers, and poor peasants of the entire gram panchayat. Our hapless father used to sit beside our bed at the dead of night and caress us, his half-asleep children, who had lost their mother only a few days back. Every single grain of rice had been used to perform the last rites of our mother. We were left at the mercy of our neighbours, who helped us have some food at least once in a day. Sarasati stopped going to school right after Mother died. Father handed over to her what little money he got as allowance from the party for working as a whole timer. Once a month, he brought a few kilograms of rice and wheat from the ration shop, which lasted for hardly a week. Every day it was a long wait for us till the evening, for Asha. She came after the toddy shop closed for the evening. She cooked rice and vegetables, which she brought with her, boiled the little milk she managed for me from unknown sources, washed the utensils, and left, after putting us to bed. All the while, Sarasati moved along, following her at every step, sat by her side when she cooked, and talked nonstop, reporting to her about what she had heard and from whom. I lay in her lap, in the cosy comfort of her soft warm body, till I fell asleep. Father usually returned late and sat by the bed side. We vaguely remembered a voice saying something incoherently till Asha forced him to retire for the night. She usually left only after we all fell asleep.

However, the mutually convenient arrangement crumbled one night. I was burning up with high fever; Karma Budhi along with few other women from our neighbourhood visited in the afternoon. They suggested that Hadam should consult an *ojha* (witch doctor) immediately to diagnose the root cause of the fever. Sanatan Manjhi came with a paste of vermilion and smeared it on my temple, placed an iron sickle under my pillow, and left with creases upon his forehead.

Grandfather snored after consuming a pot of *handiya* in the evening and Sarasati, sitting beside me, wept helplessly. Asha reached late, but took control of the situation immediately. Without waiting for Hari, she went out to collect *shiuli* leaves and administered the juice extracted from it to bring down the temperature. She decided to stay back for the night. A much relieved Sarasati fell asleep within minutes due to sheer exhaustion. Asha warded off her fatigue by vigorously rubbing her eyes, and continued replacing the soaked piece of cloth on my forehead. The fever started receding.

By the time Hari returned, it must have been midnight. Asha narrated the whole situation to him, and served rice and some left over vegetable stew. When asked whether she had had her dinner, she evaded the question skilfully, saying, 'You don't have to bother about me. Finish your food fast, so that I can be there with the ailing boy.'

Before Hari could swallow the first morsel, there was a commotion outside his hut. He was about to get up, but Asha signalled him not to. She tightened her girdle with the loose end of her sari and opened the door. Suddenly, vulgar abuses—'Dain!' 'Cheenar!' (Witch! Seductress!)—flew like stones towards Asha from the women gathered there.

'Lo and behold! This shameless woman is coming out from the house of a man, who's not her husband, at midnight, while wrapping her sari around her waist! Everyone knows that Hari slept with that woman on and off, but after Joba's death, they are now sharing the same bed in this house, and in the presence of their children!'

'Remember, I had told you that she is the one, who sucked life out of Joba. You did not believe it then. Now, she has entered her house and captured her man and even her children. The little boy is suffering from a mysterious fever. His face has turned black. I have myself seen the scratch mark on his neck.'

What followed came from the men present there, and was much more sinister: 'This woman is a threat to the entire *dahi* (habitat). She has been coming to our village since long. Who knows how many lives were lost due to her *dahani vidya* (witchcraft)? She must be taught a lesson today so that she never dares to enter our *dahi dangar*.'

Asha rushed to the verandah and shouted, 'Come on! If anyone dares to touch me, I shall kill him. Where were you all these days when these two motherless children were alone in dark nights lying on empty stomachs? They would have died by now, hadn't I promised Joba on her funeral pyre that I shall take care of them. And you pigs call me *dain*! Where was Hari all this evening? Look at that half-dead old haggard Hadam lying there unconscious... Aah!'

Someone had hit her with a stone. A shrill cry reverberated throughout the village, '*Maar*! *Maar*! Drag this witch out of the hut! Kill her.'

They were closing in on Asha. It was a matter of a few more minutes before she was lynched. Her voice choked in fear. She couldn't recognize the faces. Everything before her eyes became a blur. She stared at them vacantly, while wiping out the blood trickling down from her forehead to her left cheek.

Suddenly the shrill cry stopped. She looked back on hearing a foot step. A dark shadow was approaching. Tears rolled down and diluted the blood stain. She was about to slump when two hands clamped around her waist. She hugged him with all her might. Two little hands touched her left hand softly. Asha came out of her stupor with the support of Hari's strong hands. She stooped and picked Sarasati up in one jerk, and hugged her tightly. Hari lifted her face up, looked straight into her eyes and asked her aloud, so that everyone could hear—'Asha, be their mother and take care of that old man, or else they will not survive. Will you?'

Asha did not reply. She stared at him vacantly, tears welling up in her eyes. Sarasati entwined her neck with both hands and buried her face upon her shoulder. The crowd also stood in front of them in deafening silence.

It was to be a simple *sindur dan* ceremony at noon. When a man rubs vermilion on the parting of hair of an unmarried woman with her consent, in full public view, often during a festival or in a village fair, and both of them walk away together, the marriage is solemnized. But this time it was an inter-community marriage between a Santhal and a Shabar widow. Had it not been Hari and Asha, two rebel faces of the village, there would have been a blood-bath. They belonged to the party first and the community later.

From early morning, people started to drop in from far and near. Knowing the condition of the two family's resources, the neighbours pooled in whatever *handiya* was left in each house, supplemented by a few pots of the famous brew of Budha, the bride's father. Both Budha and Hadam were busy men. They would drink a glass of *handiya* offered by anyone. Hari's comrades arranged rice and pork out of nowhere. A couple of young fellows brought madal and *dhamsa* and started dancing. When the sun reached mid sky, women escorted Asha out in the courtyard, draped in a simple sari, but she refused to leave the child wrapped in a small *kantha*, perhaps stitched by Joba months back in anticipation. She carried the child with one hand upon her breast, and also held Sarasati's hands with the other. Kanan and Paran, obstinately drunk, insisted on dressing up the middle-aged *dular* (bridegroom) who was as nervous as a teenager. A yellow turban adorned his head with a twig of blood red Krishnachura flowers along with a few leaves tucked in, white cloth flowing from his shoulders covered his bare chest, and a dhoti was tightly wrapped around his waist.

While Paran started beating the *dhamsa* he had brought where Asha was standing, Kanan and Sanatan danced with madals hanging from their necks to usher in the groom. Hari came out holding a brass pot with his left hand and went straight towards Asha in long strides, leaving the merry makers behind. He picked up a handful of vermilion and doused it on her forehead amidst the full throated cries of the people around and the wild beating of drums.

# The Football Match

Kanchan was running with the ball at break-neck speed through the left flank. The players of Traffic School, Kharagpur, ran behind him desperately to intercept him. The sharp pricks of their studs opened several blood pores on his naked feet, often unintended, but at times, deliberate.

The elders often advised the men before the pig is let loose during festivals, 'The hunter's eyes should relentlessly follow his prey; he shouldn't mind the thorns when chasing an animal; after all, the kill will be his at the end...' Kanchan recalled.

The Traffic School players had studs in their boots. They had been wearing boots from the day they started playing football and they knew how and when to use them.

'Bear the pricks of the studs if you want to play the game, or quit!' Ranjit Sir often told them.

His two hands, spread like the wings of a fighter cock, fended him from any attempt of side-tackle; he dribbled past one, then another, and jumped over the full back sliding towards him, targeting his legs to stop him, or at least deflect the ball. At last, he was face to face with the lanky goalkeeper, helpless like a hare cornered in its hole. Kanchan leaned towards left. The goalkeeper dived to his right in anticipation, to block the shot. Kanchan flicked the ball with his right toe and rushed past the goal post to collect the ball entangled in the net.

'Goal! Goal!' screamed the handful of teachers and students of Vivekananda Vidyabhavan, Narayanpur, present in SERA Stadium in that historic moment. A pall of gloom descended in the western gallery of the stadium. The Traffic School students, their family members, and the local people from Kharagpur had occupied that side, leaving the eastern gallery to others. Several seconds passed after the whistle signalled the goal. A collective sigh ranted the air, and the crowd slumped down on the wooden gallery with frustration writ large on their faces.

Some of the Narayanpur players standing in the dugout rushed into the field. Kanchan was lying on the ground, amidst a huddle of ten other players. The referee blew the whistle repeatedly to resume the game. Ranjit Sir ran along the side line towards the huddle and shouted, 'Get down to the game! Hurry up!' The players got up, and ran to their respective positions. The play resumed for the final few minutes left. Upen Mandi, our goalkeeper, bravely faced the shots coming towards the goal in torrents and defended his territory. At last, a long whistle signalled the end of the play.

Narayanpur erupted in joy. Vivekananda Vidyabhavan, their little known school in this small town at the southern border of Bengal, lifted the Inter-School Champions Trophy of Midnapur district. The creaking Bedford truck, running since the '50s, ferried the team, a few teachers, and fewer students, who were lucky enough to find a place in the bus. When it entered Babulpur, it was already late evening. Within a few minutes, a mob of students and people from nearby localities, waiting anxiously in front of the school building, surrounded the truck. Rathikanta Mahato, the captain, held the trophy aloft and we all shouted 'hip hip hooray' at the top of our voices.

The two heroes of the day obviously were Upen, the goalkeeper, who had saved at least three scorchers from the Traffic School forwards, and Kanchan, the scorer of the lone goal of the match. However, they were the only two, who stood like zombies in the middle of the celebrating mob, as if they could not believe that they could be the centre of any celebration. Local dignitaries like the BDO saheb (the block development officer) and Daroga saheb, escorted by Chittaranjan babu, the Headmaster, had come there to join the celebration. When they came to meet the team, Head Sir shook hands with each of the members, but hugged only Kanchan and Upen. He had already heard about the exploits of the two heroes of his school. The BDO and Daroga saheb also shook their hands vigorously, but even after that, Upen and Kanchan stood there like statues with vacant looks on their faces. The adulations could not bring out any reaction from them. Ranjit Sir, the sports teacher of the school, stepped in, and said,

'Kanchan and Upen, come! Touch their feet and seek their blessings.' Both of them carried out his instructions in a robotic manner.

Ranjit babu turned towards the dignitaries and said, 'Sir, the entire team fought like tigers, but these two were outstanding. Nobody thought that we could beat Traffic School. They have been preparing for this tournament for almost a year. South Eastern Railways sponsored the team, and met all the expenses including that of a coach from Kolkata. Those players were equipped with full football gears like boots with spikes, shin guards, and had been trained by a qualified football coach. Our boys matched them, point by point, with sheer determination and endurance; where our boys excelled at was the stamina. The city boys couldn't match them in speed, or strength, during the last quarter of the game.'

The teachers, students, and players—all of them merely nodded together in agreement.

Ranjit babu, our maths teacher, doubled up as the sports teacher of the school, because of his brilliant record as a local footballer, and his passion for the game. He was the main inspiration behind grooming up selected students for the school team, working relentlessly with these raw talents for years. Today they had reached the pinnacle of glory at the district level. Obviously, after such a great success of his boys, Ranjit babu was unstoppable. Despite the frown on the Headmaster's face, he went on: 'These boys could have performed much better, if we could provide them with some instruments for exercise, and football gears.'

BDO saheb had been a football player himself in his student days, and being a Ghoti from Kolkata, he was a staunch Mohun Bagan fan. He quipped, 'I know, I know. Before independence, our Mohun Bagan Club defeated the British footballers, playing barefoot. It is your zeal to achieve something which takes you forward. You should inspire your students to make a mark in the game, get selected for the district team, and then play for Mohun Bagan Club in Kolkata, the Mecca of Indian football.'

Chittaranjan Banerjee, the Headmaster, was a 'Bangal' and belonged to the opposite camp of BDO saheb, as far as football was concerned. He was a staunch supporter of the East Bengal Club. He snidely remarked, 'Those days will never come back. Where does Mohun Bagan Club stand today in Indian football? Modern football requires proper football gears, training, and of course, skills! Sir, if you sanction a little fund to our school out of your Tribal Area Development Fund, I can arrange boots, shin guard, stockings, and other football equipment for them. I can also give some monetary assistance to our Adivasi players to meet their hostel expenses. These two boys, Upen and Kanchan, come all the way from Babulpur on foot, every day. They also work in the fields during the sowing and harvesting seasons. I shall talk to their guardians to let them stay in the hostel. I can convince them, only if I can meet the expenses from our own sources. To ask them to pay for the hostel will be preposterous.'

BDO saheb had lost his enthusiasm by then. He nodded his head, and said, 'I shall try my best. Let's see.' He left with his entourage a few minutes later, and with a collective sigh of relief, we shouted, 'Hip, hip, hurray!'

By the time the first round of celebration was over it was already 9 o'clock. The local boys of Narayanpur town would stay in the school for some more time. Kanchan, Upen, and I, three students from Babulpur—we would have to walk down almost 4 km now. The only bus going in that direction, 'Raghunath', had already left Narayanpur in the evening. Biren babu, the Hostel Super, was magnanimous enough that evening. Maintaining his characteristic frown and wry smile, he flouted his own order that hung on the notice board declaring, 'Outsiders not allowed in the hostel at night, under any circumstances'. He offered us his hospitality for that night. He also mentioned that the hostel was celebrating the win with rice and chicken curry in place of the routine lentil soup called 'daler jhol' and pumpkin. But none of us dared to accept it. We were damn sure of a tough time at home and a possible ban on our joining the team in future outstation games, if we didn't return immediately.

Since I was the youngest of the lot, Ranjit babu entrusted the responsibility of my safe return to Kanchan and Upen. I was quite relieved that Baba hadn't sent anyone on cycle to Narayanpur to take me back. He might have expected that the school would make some arrangement to drop us home, if it was too late. It would have been embarrassing for me to leave Kanchan and Upen, if I went back pillion riding, on cycle.

We walked at a brisk pace to reach home as early as possible. It was already dark. Moreover, the food packet given to us, the players, after the match, only added to our hunger after the 90 minutes of tough game. The pangs of hunger pricked us harder, once the euphoria was over.

As soon as we crossed the huts at the outskirts of the town of Narayanpur, a thin spread of shrubs and bushes shrouded in mist appeared like scattered outposts standing guard at the border, but they looked like palm-leaf soldiers because of their loneliness in the dim moonlight. We walked past the small trees and bushes and entered the kingdom of giants, the tamarind, *krishnachura,* and *shirish* trees, along the ancient Jagannath Puri Road. The trees stood silently in darkness, their leaves swaying in unison with the gentle breeze, resulting in a murmur, as if they were speaking with each other in whispers. The crescent moon played hide and seek from within the foliage, as if it was a match between the black Adivasis and the brown Dikus of Narayanpur School. The moon would eventually slide down to the other side of the sky as the night progressed, and darkness would reclaim its territory. The dark night was destined to concede defeat at the end of the game, when the sun would appear in the east.

Far ahead of us, we saw a fire, possibly that of a pyre burning in the cremation ground of Laj Pur, mid-way between Babulpur and Narayanpur. I held Kanchan's hand tightly. The cremation ground is the playground of ghosts, particularly for the spirits of those local people, whose last rites had been performed there. Who knows who all might be waiting there for us? Kanchan laughed loudly and asked, 'Are you afraid, Babu?' Sarasati had disclosed my nickname 'Babu' to her friends after she joined our school, which caught the fancy of my friends as well. I tried to say 'no' emphatically, but my voice trembled.

'Don't be afraid! I am there with you. I have seen ghosts many times since my childhood. But I know for sure that they cannot harm anyone, unless the person himself is afraid. That's why they try to instil fear in us. And remember another thing! As long as you are with me, you need not worry. I am wearing an amulet around my waist since my childhood, containing pieces of bones and claws of a bear, the protector of our clan. No evil spirit can touch me.' It struck me then that he was the grandson of Sanatan Manjhi, the most powerful priest of the Adivasis in this part of Narayanpur.

After this double assurance, I became bold enough to leave his hand and ask, 'Kanchan, how were those ghosts? Did you see them clearly?'

Kanchan was mighty pleased with the question. He answered with conviction, 'Oh! So many of them! The ghosts I have seen are mostly the spirits of those persons, who died unnatural deaths. Just a few days back, I stayed a bit late in the hostel with my friends. It was already dark when I was crossing the lonely stretch before the Saheb Bungalow. Suddenly, I saw a rabbit crossing the road in front of me. It vanished the next moment, and there appeared a woman draped in a white sari under the Shaora tree. I recognized her immediately; that was Basanti, Bhola's wife; that was the place where she was cremated after she hanged herself. Then, a few days after that, on the last full moon night, I was coming back from Saheb Bangalow after meeting Dasho and other friends. I was a few metres from the Babui Bridge. From there I saw something lying on the road and howling like a dying dog. I thought, maybe a truck had run over a stray dog. Suddenly, I remembered that it was the same place, where Paran had been hacked to death. I ran towards the rail line for my life, and crossed the rail bridge over Babui to reach home. Next morning, I went there and checked. No trace of dog or any other animal was there, but the tar on that spot was still wet. Again, there was that—'

Suddenly, Upen slapped Kanchan hard and shouted at the top of his voice, 'Will you stop all this bull shit? Here and now! Don't you see so many living ghosts and witches around you, more dangerous than the dead ones?' Realizing his misbehaviour, he added a few seconds later, 'Oh my god! Damn! Forget it! We are already late. Tomorrow we have to reach the school early for the special assembly. Walk faster now!' Kanchan did not utter another word.

Both Kanchan and I realized our mistake. Upen was otherwise very cool and never lost his temper, but the name of Paran had touched a raw nerve, and that was why he reacted in this manner. Paran was his uncle through a distant relation. Like many others, he also idolized Paran from his childhood. Paran was among those few

Adivasi boys, who passed the fourth class from the village school and went to High School. Upen also saw from very close quarters, the sufferings of Paran and his family, the sudden demise of his mother, the prolonged illness of his father, which forced him to drop out and become a labourer to earn whatever little he could to sustain himself and his father. And then came his political adventure, which resulted in his cruel death. Years later, when I heard the story of Paran's journey from Upen, we wept together.

My house was in the middle of Babulpur. Just when we reached the outskirts of Babulpur, we saw flashes of torch lights coming towards us. We rightly guessed that the search party was for me. Kanchan ruffled my hair and said, 'Babu, the wounds on my legs are hurting. I have to put the paste of "Ravan lata" leaves on those for quick healing. I may not be able to go to school tomorrow. Tell our class teacher, if he asks.' I caught hold of his hand, and whispered in his ears, 'Kanchan, Sarasati will wait for us. If you happen to go that side on the way to your house, tell her.' Kanchan smiled and nodded his head before taking a few hurried steps to be as far away as possible before the men arrived. He was singing a song I had heard earlier and knew whom he was singing it for:

*'Aam ma chetan kulhi janum buta*
*Eoin ma latar kulhi jojbuta*
*Jojom tite katuboh suyud ayme*
*Alang yanpam dore dah lo ghatre...'*
[You are standing under the berry tree of your village
And I am here under the tamarind tree.
But, on hearing the first note of your flute
I shall be with you on the banks of the river.]

Upen waved at me, but didn't say anything. From a distance I looked back and saw that both of them were limping. I had seen the wounds on their toes and feet. They would take a turn now towards Babui Bridge, cross over, and enter the dark alley of the Adivasi Para.

They would have to walk a long way and cross Babui Bridge to reach their huts engulfed in darkness. The news of their heroics and the great victory for the school would not be of much relevance to them once they reach their hut, as irrelevant to them are the lighted streets and houses of Narayanpur, the SERA Stadium, and the celebration. Their mothers would be awake, as usual, with a plate of rice and *sajne* leaves fried in little or no oil, and their fathers would be snoring away the blues of mahua. Half empty stomachs will trouble the boys more today, after the grueling, 90-minute-long game. Yet they will not ask for more rice, because they know that their mothers might have already skipped dinner so that the sons could eat. They would regret playing the game which aggravates the pangs of hunger; they would regret ignoring the advice of the elders—'Do something that fetches you something to fill your belly; how long will you be able to run around on the ground kicking a piece of leather on empty stomach?' But I know, they will still play the game ignoring the wounds, ignoring the emaciated bodies of their parents, their siblings, or even hunger. It is their new found identity: proven ability to bring laurels for their school, their village, their country.

# The Cauldron on Fire

It was the end of spring and the onset of summer, time to plough the land to make it ready for sowing paddy as soon as the rain comes. This was also the time to settle which plot of land was to be retained by the owner, and which he would pass on for sharecropping. Unless some action was taken to establish the ownership by ploughing the land, the peasants would have to wait for another year. The established norm was that whoever sowed the seed would reap the harvest. Landowners started mobilizing labourers to plough the land in their possession, leaving very little for the sharecroppers during this uncertain time. Small farmers were categorically told that this year, they would not get to sow paddy in the land that they had been sharecropping for so long.

The first one to get the axe was Bhola. On the morning of Akshay Tritiya, the most auspicious day to begin the year's farming, Bhola and Basanti reached the piece of land he had sharecropped for Balai Chowdhury in Matiyal. Even from a distance he could clearly see a few people ploughing his piece of land. He dropped his plough, and ran towards the field. Prankrishno was standing on the skirting under an umbrella, supervising labourers ploughing his land. Bhola shouted, 'What are you doing here? I am the *bhag chashi* (sharecropper) of this plot.'

Prankrishno smugly said, 'No. From this year we have decided to take it back from you and cultivate it ourselves.'

Bhola pounced upon the first man with the plough and pushed him away. He was unbridling the bullocks, when Prankrishno and his men caught hold of his hand. They pinned him down on the ground and rained upon him lathis, which they were carrying for driving the bullocks. Basanti pushed the people surrounding Bhola and threw herself upon him. She managed to shield Bhola by taking some of the blows upon herself. Prankrishno's men stopped, but he himself pulled her apart, wrenching her hands out of the grip of Bhola. He slapped Basanti several times shouting, '*Shali*! *Randi*! Aren't you sleeping these days with that bastard Adivasi, Paran? Call him! Let me see how he saves your husband, and the land.'

The insinuation was enough for Bhola to forget his precarious condition. With desperate efforts, he sprang to his feet, shoved Basanti away, to keep her out of harm's way. His fist found its mark. The moment blood oozed out from Prankrishno's nose, he started howling at the top of his voice,

'Bhola! Bhola wants to kill me. See, what he has done to me! Catch him and tie him up. He has to be handed over to the police.' By the time his men tied his hands, people working in the neighbouring fields heard the cry, and rushed in. Basanti's voice of protest drowned in the milieu. Blood clots on Prankrishno's nose, lips, and chin clenched the issue in his favour.

Bhola could not believe that even after their party had come to power, these *jotdars* would dare to do such things. He commanded Basanti: 'Run, Basanti, run! Find out Paran, Hari, or Kanan, and tell them what has happened.'

Then, turning towards Prankrishno and his men, he shouted, 'Leave this plot of land. This land has been with us since my grandfather's time. I shall file my claim for *barga* on this land. It is now *our* government. We will have justice.'

Prankrishno handed out a tight slap. 'Haven't you sent your wife to your leaders right now!' shouted Prankrishno, and then, added in a hushed voice, 'Let us also see what they can do for you and your wife. You can get back this land, only if you can produce the paper in your name. Do you have anything to prove that you have been the sharecropper of this plot ever in the past? Show it here, or else, I shall make you lame for life.'

Basanti ran towards the newly constructed party office in the middle of Babulpur, as fast as she could. It was only a small hut with a thatched roof and a bamboo door, but the house was at the heart of the Bengali Para of Babulpur. The day after the party came to power, workers had occupied the vacant plot and had erected the hut in 24 hours. Luckily, Paran was present there. He listened to her patiently. He knew that retaliation was going to come sooner or later, but he had not anticipated that they would strike where it hurt the most, that they would use the ignorance of the poor sharecroppers to dispossess them of the land under sharecropping.

Paran asked a boy sitting there to lock the door and leave the key with Gobindo at the tea stall. He walked so fast that Basanti could not keep pace with him. She ran fast to catch up. Holding his hand, she said, 'Paran, don't go there alone. They are out to take revenge upon you. They are waiting for you, not Bhola.'

Paran smiled and said. 'Don't worry. Let them do whatever they like, but I cannot leave Bhola alone.'

It was another recap of the story, played so often in the past. Once you dare to confront the fear, it melts away. Paran reached there and caught hold of the first man in front of him by his neck and inflicted a severe blow on his face. The man fell flat on the ploughed land. Paran shouted at the next man he confronted from a distance and said,

'Come on! Hit me, if you can!'

The man was visibly nervous and looked at Prankrishno for the next step. Before he could react, Paran dealt another blow to him. He staggered and fell. Now, it was Prankrishno, who was facing him, with fear writ large on his face. Paran did not touch him. With so far unknown authority, he sternly said, 'Leave Bhola here, and run away from this plot of land! It is Bhola's land. Anyone, who dares to put a foot over it, will face the consequences.'

Prankrishno flinched and his men retracted their steps. They remained silent when Paran untied the hands of Bhola, but the helpless anger in Prankrishno's eyes would have turned Paran into ashes, had it been the times written about in the *Ramayana*, or even the *Mahabharata*. These days one never knows what will happen where these savage Adivasis are involved; whether the police will take the side of the party in power, or do justice to the owner of the land for having all papers in order. After Prankrishno and his men left Bhola's field, Paran instructed Bhola,

'Don't leave the field before you plough it at least once. Call the people of your village in the evening, all the sharecroppers and peasants. I shall be there. Unless all of you stand together, you don't have a chance. Prankrishno will go to the police station and file a report. We must have one or two witnesses, who will say that you have been cultivating the land since the last ten years.'

The people came in hordes: the sharecroppers and the labourers to whom the party had promised a new social order. They themselves identified the plot of land to be taken over from the *jotdar* once the current or past sharecroppers submitted their claim and the locals verified it. Next morning they marched to the plot carrying ploughs, bullocks, and red flags. Others joined these processions, shouted 'Inquilab Zindabad', and ploughed the land in the hope that their turn will also come. In the past, they had been victimized for their allegiance to the party by their employers. Now, with the loans drying up, seeds out of reach of the small farmers, and the dwindling demand for labourers, all of them knew that the situation could become worse than the past years of Congress rule. Hari, Kanan, Paran, and even Bhola knew that if no action was taken by the party immediately, things would go out of hand, but there was no signal from the leaders. Every time there was an incident of forcible dispossession of land, the police came and asked all to maintain peace. It was status quo that they maintained.

Hari was compelled to convene a Krishak Sabha meeting in the evening at the Primary School building of Babulpur. He also informed Sudhi babu, Prabhat, and Bijon about the meeting along with a stern message that everyone should be present in the meeting.

Sudhi Master felt slighted. He was the secretary of the local committee, but the agenda of the meeting had been set by Krishak Sabha. He decided to take things in his own hand from the beginning and initiated the discussion: 'We are very much worried about the situation; but we also know that being in the government has thrust upon us a greater responsibility. We should keep the larger interest of the party in view, rather than what has happened to a sharecropper here and there. There should be some discipline in the party. No one should be allowed to take law into their own hands. Bhola physically assaulted Prankrishno. He has lodged an FIR along with a medical report. How can we support Bhola? He should have submitted an application to the party office about the violation of his right as a sharecropper. The party would have taken appropriate action. Now, he has to face the consequences. Comrade Jyoti Basu is the Home Minister and responsible for law and order. Alright! But we cannot take law in our hand. We should not do anything that can malign his name and the party's. Paran is repeatedly indulging in such rash decisions. Either he should mend his ways, or part his way with the party.'

Hari did not recuperate fully from the shocking death of Joba even after so many days. But that old spark still remained in him. He addressed Sudhi directly, 'Comrade, we flaunt our power as leaders for the people. If we don't stand by them, they will also desert us. They are illiterate people. So am I. We don't understand all these things called law, order, and court. If one sows the seed in a plot of land, it is his for the year. Had I been in Bhola's or Paran's situation, I would have done the same thing, or even worse; I would have kicked their balls so hard that they wouldn't have dared to go near others' lands for life.'

There was pin-drop silence in the room. After a while, Sudhi got up and said, 'If you have no regard for law and party discipline, then I should not be here. I shall report the matter to the Local Committee. Let them take a decision.'

When he was leaving, somebody quipped from behind, 'Are you going to have a cup of tea with Naren babu or Prankrishno now? Please go and ask them not to evict their sharecroppers till the Barga rights are settled.'

Sudhangshu turned back as if he was stung by a bee and shouted, 'Who? Who said this? Come forward! Tell this once more, if you have the guts.'

Paran got up. He moved a few steps forward towards Sudhangshu, and said, 'Comrade, whoever has said this meant no offence to you. *Jotdar*s are evicting *bargadar*s everywhere. We have to stop it. If this can be done through negotiation, alright; otherwise, the party must take the side of the *bargadar*s, and not the landlords. The peasants must get their land back by hook or by crook. Let the law or the order, so dear to you, go to hell!'

Prabhat and Bijon had been silent so long, but now they got the opportunity to pin down Paran, and also give a befitting reply to Hari. Bijon screamed, 'Paran! Shut up! You are talking like those renegades, who divided the party. They believe in anarchy in the name of revolution. That could destroy the party so painfully built up by our leaders. Are you in touch with them? Comrade Hari, we must nip this kind of indiscipline in the bud.'

They got up and joined Sudhangshu at the door step of the party office. Hari looked at them and said in a stern voice, 'Wait!' All three of them looked back and retracted their step. Like all the others sitting in the room, they were also stunned to hear Hari's voice at this pitch. Hari looked around the room. He knew all of them very well. They represented the people of their respective areas in the Krishak Sabha, but their first commitment was towards their own people, and not the party. Every small development taking place here would be blown up, when it would reach the people at the village level and be discussed in details. So far they have been watching the in-fighting within the party without any apparent reaction.

Hari had been using a khaki half pant and a *ganjee* outside since the days he used to pull a rickshaw. Today he wore a vest in addition to preside over the meeting. Others were in short dhotis, some of them carried a *gamcha* on their neck, which they used for wiping out sweat and driving away mosquitoes. Hari saw that for the first time, Bhola, Khudi, and a few other Bengali comrades were sitting there along with the Adivasis, but they neither reacted to the outburst of Sudhi babu, nor spoke anything in his favour so far. He turned towards Paran and said, 'Paran! Behave yourself! You should not talk to Sudhi babu in this manner. Sit down!'

Then he looked at Sudhangshu, and said calmly, 'Comrade, these illiterate people do not know how to talk. They are also scared that their land will be taken away. That's why they have lost their head. But we have to address their concerns also. Let us call the landowners of each village separately and request them to maintain the status quo of each plot of land for this year.'

Thereafter he addressed the people sitting silent so far and said, 'What do you say?'

The reaction was surprising: 'Hari bhai, the landlords of Ranipur are desperately trying to get their lands back from the *bargadars*,' said Rupu from Ranipur.

Blacksmith Naran added, 'We know that they are afraid of the party. This is the time when we should strike the iron, when it is hot.'

Supai shouted from the back, 'We will fight till the end, and won't leave our share of the land, but the way you people from the party are behaving, I doubt whether you want that or not. Tell me Sudhi babu, how many times did you meet Nagen babu, and how many times you have come to us?'

Sudhi babu could not control himself after hearing these. He took a step back; coming back to his place in the middle, he addressed Hari, 'Comrade Hari! I think, you have erred in your judgement. Some people here are cleverer than you think. They are instigating people to insult the leaders, blaming them of inaction, insinuating them with false allegations. Let me tell you clearly, whatever I am doing is according to the party line.'

Hari tried to pacify him. 'Sudhi babu, please do not be angry. I apologize on behalf of everybody here. These illiterate peasants don't understand politics. They want a few *cottahs* of land to sow seeds and grow a little paddy to fill their bellies. They have lost their patience on seeing that even after the party coming to power, nothing has been happening in their favour. Let us find out some way to reassure these peasants.'

Sudhi realized that Hari had cleverly turned the table. He got up and said, 'Well, these things cannot be discussed here. You come to the Narayanpur party office tomorrow. We will work out some plan.' Without waiting for a response, he hurriedly left with Prabhat and Bijon.

Hari came back from Narayanpur the next evening with a grim face and headed straight to Budha's shop. Kanan, Supai, and Paran huddled around him. He explained the gist of discussions in the party office.

'The Local Committee leaders were unanimous in their decision that Paran should be expelled from the party. I explained the situation to them, and said that it is not Paran's fault. The people of Babulpur are facing starvation. If we don't do anything, they may go to any extreme, but Sudhi babu wouldn't listen. It may happen any day that some letter will be sent expelling him. Paran, don't do anything to aggravate the situation. I need some time to talk to Sukumar babu to resolve the issue.'

Supai was more pragmatic, or maybe he had a foreboding of things to come; he caught hold of Hari's hand and said, 'Hari bhai, Paran is now the enemy of *jotdars* as well as some leaders of our own party. He is such a fool that he has also antagonized Sudhi babu. Once this information reaches the *jotdars*, they will try to eliminate him because he has inflicted maximum damage upon them.'

Kanan agreed with him. He touched Paran's shoulder, and said, 'Paran, keep a low profile for some time. The party is our strength, and it represents a group of people with the same agenda, the same goal. If you are identified as an individual on a mission alone, the attack will be aimed at you. Take people along with you to get things done, even if it delays your actions.'

Paran wanted to say something, but Hari silenced him, 'Paran, it is my decision that you will not move alone at night, even for the party's work. Consult Kanan, or me before you do anything.'

Paran took a dirty red folded paper out of his pocket. He moved towards the only kerosene lamp placed in the middle belching out more smoke than light and started reading:

'Which road to take in the revolution is a fundamental question affecting its success, or failure. The revolution must take the path of relying on peasants, establishing base areas in the countryside, persisting in protracted armed struggle, and using the country side to encircle, and finally capture the cities. This is Mao Tsetung's way, the way that has led the Chinese revolution to victory, and the only way to victory for the revolution of all oppressed nations and people...'

There was absolute silence in the room, till it was broken by Paran again. 'This was a leaflet that I got from Ranipur Adivasi Para last night,' said Paran. Subhas bhai and two unknown young men had visited the *para* the night before, but no one informed me on that night. Something is brewing, Hari Kaka. People have lost their trust on us. We will alienate the peasants further, if we still dither. Now, it is for you to decide what you want to do. I shall continue to do what I am doing because, I know that I am right.' Paran got up abruptly and left the room.

Rupu moved closer to Hari and whispered, 'They were very critical about the attitude of the party after winning the election and called us opportunists, hungry for power, and a word "burjua" (bourgeois), the meaning of which I don't understand. They are also planning something sinister. It is a secret that they didn't divulge to anyone, but it was very clear from the way they were asking people about the landlords of the village.'

Everybody was looking at Hari, but he remained silent. The meeting was inconclusive. After everybody else left, Hari asked, 'Kanu, Budha's shop must be open still. Let's take a round. Paran may be there. I need to talk to him.' When they reached there, they found the shop empty and silent, as it should have been at that time of the night in Babulpur.

# The Killing Field

I still remember that sultry morning. Clouds hung very low in the sky as if they would descend on the earth at any moment. There was no sign of the sun on the eastern horizon. The moment I got up from bed and came out of our house in the morning, I sensed a chilly wind blowing from nowhere. When I saw that nobody was inside, I came out through the main door, and saw people standing on the road in groups discussing something in hushed tones; women had assembled near the well, and were whispering to each other. My ears caught part of a sentence, '...murdered just across Babui Bridge,' and for the first time in my short span of life, I tasted fear—a taste, which chills the stomach, and goes down the intestines right up to the anus. Slowly, I caught up with the details. Last night, some unidentified people hacked Paran to death in an isolated spot near Babui Bridge, when he was on his way back to his hut in Adivasi Para.

More shock was in store for me in school. Dasarath, Suren, and Kanchan were absent. Upen came, but throughout the first half, he was sitting with his face down, almost touching the desk. During lunch break, he was surrounded by curious teachers and students alike, but he did not utter a single word. When pestered to the limit, he snapped—'What do you want to hear? Yes, he was killed. Who killed him, I don't know. Why? I don't know.'

Paran was known as a man of action among the insiders of the party as well as the people outside. The incidents of brawls he was involved in, during the short period he worked for the party, were reason enough to brand him as the perennial dissenter within the party. He didn't believe in niceties of looking into pros and cons before taking any action. Whenever he came to know about any threat or harm to the supporters of the party, he jumped into action. He led people from the front, and never shied away from physically intervening on the spot. In this side of Babulpur, we heard many stories of his ruthless ways of handling situations. Everyone still remembered the incidence of the violent clash he had had with Prankrishno and his men, a week before the election. That was the turning point of the assembly election, not only in this village, but also in other parts of the constituency.

After United Front came to power, Paran became very active. He identified *benami* and surplus lands with the help of the old hands of landlords. I witnessed him leading party processions armed with bows, arrows, and spears. He would wear only a dusty short dhoti and a shirt, and would carry a red flag on his shoulder, and march on the Babulpur road to take possession of the *benami* or government land identified by them. They would forcibly plough the land, put a red flag on a pole, and erect it on the plot as a mark of the party's possession. No one dared to question his actions. Young Adivasis loved him, but the people living north of Babui River were scared. Everyone knew that the big farmers, who had lost the land they had possessed for long, were livid with anger, but Paran's brutal death was a bolt from the blue for the entire village. It was one political murder which shook entire Narayanpur Thana and had impact beyond its boundaries, but the murder was the culmination of many small incidents of violence, which had polluted the air much before the incident took place.

The euphoria of coming to power for the first time by a Communist Party didn't last long. Comrade Sukumar Sengupta, the District Secretary of Midnapur, called prominent workers of the entire Narayanpur block for forming the Local Committee in the block, and a Branch Committee in every Anchal Panchayat. Sudhi babu asked Hari, Kanan, Kartik, and Paran to come, but when it came to forming the Branch Committee for Babulpur, they were surprised to hear the names of Prabhat and Bijon, two young men, known more for their daring attempts to muzzle the check post officials and the police, and to smuggle rice from Odissa. They were also infamous for their drunken brawls in roadside mahua dens, rather than their role in the peasants' agitation for higher wages, or for the rights of sharecroppers. The Branch Committee was formed with Sudhi babu as Secretary, and Prabhat, Bijon, Kanan, and Hari as its members. Hari was made the president of Krishak Sabha, the peasants' wing of the party; but considering his physical and mental condition after the sudden death of his wife, Joba, Hari was to be assisted by Paran in discharging his responsibilities.

In a meeting of the Local Committee, Paran addressed none other than Sukumar babu, the District Secretary himself, and asked: 'Comrade, now that we are in power, can we immediately take up the task of identifying *benami* lands, and redistribute them among the landless in the locality?'

Sukumar babu remained silent for a while; then answered in a low voice, 'Of course, comrade! But I would advise you to be cautious. Do you think a coalition government, in which our party is only one among fourteen, can bring revolution? This is an opportunity to do your ground work. Go to the peasants, the labourers, the sharecroppers! Tell them to rally under the red flag! Build up the Krishak Sabha in your branch, till the party is an integrated part of the government. The uprising of the peasants and the workers is still far off. Revolution is still afar.'

Paran interpreted Sukumar da's words in his own way. They were being asked not to destabilize the newly formed government by desisting from any effort to escalate the peasant movement; but what he could not understand was why were they representing the party in the village and mobilizing people in the hamlets, lanes, and huts, to vote for the Communist Party, in the face of attacks by rich farmers? They had promised two square meals a day to those hungry faces, had led the people to dream that once the party came to power, it would support the people's movement, it would stop the police action against poor people, and initiate speedy land reforms that would unshackle them from the vicious cycle of *dadan*. Now that the party was in power, why should the people need to suppress their hunger and anger?

If their anger did not find its outlet, it would explode. So he did not have any way out, but to ask people to get ready for the final push despite all the warnings he had received from the leaders of the party.

A shrill cry shattered the silence of the night in Babulpur a few hours later. Balai babu used to get up at four in the morning when the cock crowed for the first time; not because he was very spiritual or health conscious, but the chronic dysentery he suffered from forced him to run for life at that wee hour. If he delayed even by a second, his dhoti would get soiled; droplets would trace his route up to the place of release. He was following his routine that night, and someone followed him to the corner plot far away from the house and hacked him from behind. The cry that goes out from the body when the soul leaves it transcends the power of the vocal cord. Bipin babu's voice pierced the walls of his house, the barriers of trees, and rung in the ears of everyone awake or asleep in Babulpur.

Those who assembled near the dead body looked more at the torn pieces of the Bangla newspaper on which shined the letters written with vermilion-red color, 'Comrade Mao Tse Tung Lal Selam', 'Naxal Bari jug jug jio', than the dead body itself. Among the onlookers stood Hari, Kanan, and Sudhi, who tried their best to convince the daroga that their party was as much against such killings as the Congress. But Gopal Daroga had risen from the ranks; from a mere sepoy to the position he occupied now was not because of his long years of service in the police force, but also because of his long nose, which could smell a thing from afar. He asked Prankrishno, 'Whom do you suspect? Was there any incident recently which could have led to this?'

Prankrishno grabbed this opportunity with both hands to take revenge upon Paran. He described the incident in the paddy field adding a lot of colour and also added that Paran was seen in Ranipur at midnight. When the daroga tried to pursue the lead further, Hari snubbed him, 'Paran was with us in a meeting there. Does it mean that we are also involved in this killing? What about those posters?'

Gopal Daroga didn't dare to push the theory further, ignoring the ruling party leaders. A case was registered under Section 302 IPC against unknown persons, but that added fuel to the fire burning inside Prankrishno. He couldn't believe that some unknown people had killed his father for no apparent reason. He repeatedly swore that he will teach the pigs, those who were responsible for his father's death, a lesson that no one will forget.

It was the weekly market day. Paran was seen drinking rice liquor at the southern side of the *haat*, watching cock-fight. Then people saw him talking animatedly with Basanti and Bhola. Someone, in the evening, saw him crossing Babui Bridge and going towards the Bengali Para. What happened thereafter, nobody knew for sure, but the scene recreated by most was that he had visited Bhola's house on an invitation by Bhola and Basanti, or Basanti alone. People talked about an affair of some sorts between Paran and Basanti.

However, there was no dispute about the fact that when he was coming back from the Bengali Para alone fairly late in the night, some people followed him in the cover of darkness. As soon as he crossed the Babui Bridge, they pounced on him and struck him with knives. Paran must have fought back; this was evident from the injury he got on his hands and back, but the sheer number of the killers must have been insurmountable for even Paran. He cried 'Mai gaw! Baap!' every time he got a hit. The cry reached the huts of the Adivasi Para instantly. They recognized his voice from the sloganeering he had been doing in every *michil* for the past few years. Everyone, who heard it, came out and ran towards the bridge following the cry, but by the time they reached, Paran was gasping for breath as his throat was slit neatly; his severed limbs trembling for the last time.

The horror of the night did not end there. Far away from the Babui Bridge, under the cover of the dark of night, a group of men knocked at Bhola's door. As soon as Bhola opened the door, they pounced upon him, gagged him with his own dhoti, and tied him to the bamboo pole of his own hut. Basanti was dragged out from the confines of the room and disrobed. No one in the neighbourhood dared to respond to her cries. Two persons pinned her down, pulled her legs apart, and the third one forced himself upon the dazed woman with a glee that subdued her cries. They took turns to perpetrate the same act, and left her unconscious with indelible scars all over her body. No one knew what happened thereafter. Two bodies were found hanging from the bamboo poles that supported the roof of the hut that had been so lovingly erected by the couple just a few years back.

# The Retaliation

'Long, long back, Udurdurg was elected unanimously as the king supremo of the tribesmen for his sagacity and valour.'

This was the beginning of a story Hadam told me one night, when he was in his reminiscing mood. He was a master storyteller with unending stock of stories about kings, battles, animals, and hunters. After consuming a lion's share of the *handiya* brewed by Asha *baahu* that evening, he sat down in the verandah closing his eyes, and narrated a story told and retold by generations of elders to the next generation:

'The king, Udurgurg, lived in a fort on the top of the hills, made invincible with a high wall of stone all around and a deep trench outside, full of crocodiles and snakes. The king himself was very learned and powerful. People lived very happily in his kingdom. They harvested enough grain from the fertile field, clean and sweet water flowed in rivers, and the jungle was full of birds and animals. Indra, the king of the aliens, who descended from the sky, was jealous of him. He invaded the fort to dethrone Udurdurg a number of times, and to capture his kingdom, but he was defeated every time by the brave tribal army under the leadership of Udurdurg. The aliens had to flee like rats.

At last, Indra devised a plan to capture the tribal king. He engaged Durga, the most beautiful woman in his kingdom to help him invade the fort through a secret passage, so that he could capture the fort, and take King Udurdurg as hostage. One fine morning, she appeared at the gate of the fort, and requested the guards to allow her to meet the king. When Udurdurg saw her, he was mesmerized by her beauty. Durga stayed back in the fort as a consort of the king and Udurdurg eventually married her. The woman started exploring the palace and discovered the secret tunnels through which anyone could enter the fort easily. She then informed Indra about the tunnel, and also revealed the secret about the room, where the king kept his weapons. Indra attacked the fort through the tunnel and captured it. Udurdurg managed to flee with the help of his loyal soldiers, but he was so hurt knowing that his beloved had betrayed him that he became a yogi by the renunciation of worldly things and started living in the jungle like a monk. His own people remembered him while working like slaves in the kingdom of the aliens. They could not accept Indra as their king due to his misrule, and finally left for the deeper forest, where their own king resided. The woman, Durga, also realized her mistake and went to live with Udurdurg. From then onwards, the tribals remained in the jungle and worshipped him as one of their gods, the Bir. Durga deserted the aliens and stayed back as their goddess.'

Hadam slumped into stupor. He was too drunk to talk anymore. His emaciated body and deteriorating health could no longer take the physical and mental strain he had been undergoing for the last few months.

Hadam could not recognize his own people these days. The brutal killing of Paran had been forgotten so soon by everybody. Wherever one would go, one would hear people talking about land and money; every other day, people carrying red flags, lathis, spears, and bows and arrows would march into a plot of land that they would have had identified beforehand. They would hoist the flag at one corner of the land, and plough it to stake their claim. Then, people from the opposite camp would have to pay the right amount of money at the right place and reach the same plot of land, waving the tricolour. They would then bring down the red flag, and replace it with their own on the same bamboo pole. Neither the *tehshildar*, nor the Land Revenue Officer cared to verify whether it was *khas* land vested with the government, or *benami* land registered in the name of a fictitious person. Two groups of poor peasants would fight amongst themselves. The right on the piece of land was determined by money and muscle power.

Then there were Murali and Kartik, another class of people, who were very regular in the meetings and *michils* of the party, and very vociferous too. Hadam could recognize such people easily and read their intentions like the back of his palm. They would always walk in the front row of every *michil*, and sit in front of the dais of any party assembly. Hadam knew that these people were neither peasants, nor labourers. They were like jackals, who bark the whole night from behind bushes, and fall silent once they sneek into the huts to steal chicken. Hadam wondered, where was the king, whom they had elected after so much sacrifice, only a few months back? Why didn't he step in, and deliver justice to his own people?

He told Hari about all this, but did not get any response. Hadam knew in the heart of his heart that Hari was aware of it, but perhaps under some compulsion, for which he was not speaking up. He could not tell Hari about those self-seekers who had now crowded the corridors of the party office. He felt that for some reasons, Hari had lost his enthusiasm after Paran was killed. He attended the meetings, joined the *michils* as a routine, but it was clearly evident that something was brewing inside him which was beyond his grasp.

Hadam was not in a state of health to think hard for a long stretch of time. He came out of the house, and took the road leading towards the only place he thought he should go, and straightaway headed to Budha's liquor shop, singing his favourite song at the top of his voice:

*'Jomaban yuanbon rouski te bon tahena*
*Naoa hasa haram bang tahena*
*Saru sakam dah leka jeoi ma tolmol*
*Naoa hasa haram bang tahena'*
[Let us enjoy our drinks
Leaving the choice to the pitchers
This life itself is like the clay jug
Never stable like a drop of water on the hyacinth]

However, that evening, when he entered the shop, he felt that something unusual was happening there. It was not the same place where evening revellers shouted themselves hoarse on rising prices of mustard oil or salt, lack of rain, the coming festival of *Sarna*, or other such flimsy issues. Darga, Mana, Hapna, and two-three others were there as usual; Asha must have kept enamel cups in front of them with liquor or *handiya* like any other day, but they looked tense, as if they had consumed more than their quota already.

Hadam had not lost his sharp intuition even though his eyes and ears had become weak with age. He could sense that some unknown people were around. In another few seconds, he realized that something was going on behind the closed door at the end of the hut. Two young men sat in front of the door with a glass full of liquor each in their hands, but their alert eyes revealed their real intention was not consumption of liquor. Hadam did not flinch when he took his steps forward through the small gap between them. They also did not stop him. He stopped near the door for a while and realized that their eyes followed him. He opened the door for himself and entered into the backyard, where a few unknown faces, obviously young Dikus from the city, speaking to a good number of Adivasi and Bengali young men from Babulpur and nearby villages. There were a few women also, in the front row. Among them was a woman, who resembled Asha, sitting like a stone figurine with wide eyes, and gulping down every word spoken by the outsiders. Hadam had lost confidence on his eyesight at this old age. Why would Asha be there?

Hadam moved a few steps forward. He could not believe his eyes when he saw an unmistakably tall and hefty figure under the shadow of the sprawling mango tree. It was Subhas standing at the back with a few young men. He had disappeared from public eyes a year back, after his arrows grievously injured Heeru's men in the paddy field of Nuapada during labour strike. He had been declared as a proclaimed offender by the police. Hadam had seen him last in his own hut on the day his son, Hari, came back from jail. He had come under the cover of darkness, had talked to Hari in a hushed voice for some time, and had disappeared into the dark of night.

Hadam wriggled his emaciated body through the people standing behind those sitting on the mat, and sat down on the bare ground to listen to the young man with unkempt beard talking animatedly in chaste Bangla. Another young man with spectacles sat quietly in the middle, but occasionally interjected with a word or two in a hushed voice. The man with unkempt beard looked like the clown in the *jatra* staged at the temple during the autumn worship of Durga. He shouted occasionally in a quivering voice, like the clown, except that nobody laughed; he was talking about the exploitation of peasants in Naxalbari, their resistance, and the massacre of innocent people in police firing. People sat around him mesmerized, listening to his speech with rapt attention.

'Those familiar with the peasants' movement should know the truth. The peasants live and die for only one thing: their land. Therefore, the struggle is for land. Nothing more, or nothing less. The leaders told us before the election that if they came to power, they would distribute surplus land among the landless; sharecroppers would not be evicted from the land they are cultivating; rather they would be given *barga* rights. The police would not intervene in the fight between the peasants and the landlords, when it is about surplus or vested land. But is it happening in your village? Speak the truth!'

There was a loud chorus of emphatic 'No!' from the people. After a few moments' silence the young man continued:

'If we compare the situation today with the past, it will become clear. After the British left our country, the peasants of Kakdwip started the Tebhaga movement. In 1948, our own government tried to crush it using brute force. The police opened fire on unarmed men, women, and children, killing and maiming scores of innocent people. Subversive methods of dividing people in the name of revolution were applied dividing the landless and small peasants. Same thing happened after the government passed the Land Ceiling Act. It has not been implemented during the last ten years of its existence. This government, which includes the Communist parties in the coalition, is no different from the governments of the past. They are asking the people to sit quietly for some more time to get the benefits. They have forgotten that they are enjoying the power in 1967, because of the Tebhaga and Food Movement and the massive strike by tea garden workers in 1966. It was the ultimate sacrifice of Nurul Islam, Kalu Mondal, and Beeray Pradhan, and the bloody fight by hundreds of others, which paved the way for them to become ministers and MLAs from being humble workers of the Communist Party.'

Hadam was finding it difficult to sit cross-legged any longer; he found a log further back and sat comfortably to listen to the bespectacled young man speaking in a calmer voice, but spewing more fire:

'Barely a year ago, in the month of May, three months after the United Front government had come to power, the Krishak Samity of a place called Naxalbari decided to take possession of the vested land of Ishwar Tirkey, one of the very big *jotdars* of the area. Peasants in large numbers reached the field with plough and bullocks to take possession of the land by ploughing it, but Ishwar Tirkey's men, armed with lathis, swords, and spears, attacked them, and beat them up mercilessly. The peasants regrouped and surrounded the house of Ishwar Tirkey in protest. He was able to sneak out and send one of his men to the police station. Within a few hours, a large posse of policemen surrounded the peasants. They asked the peasants to lift seize. When the peasants refused, they opened fire. Agitated peasants counter-attacked with bows and arrows. One police officer, Sonam Wangdi was fatally injured, who later died in the hospital. On the next day, armed policemen surrounded the village and opened fire upon a mob comprising mostly of women and children. Eleven people were killed, among whom were eight women and two children. All this while, Communist ministers in the government, whom the workers and peasants had elected, remained silent. Ask your leaders whether what I am saying is true or false. If they have done this in Naxalbari will they do anything different here?'

He had to stop his speech. Each one of the fifty-odd people assembled there simultaneously started talking at the top of their voices. Kartik from Nuapada was hurling choicest abuses against the local leaders of the party holding them responsible for all the recent incidents of showdown with the police and *jotdars* in Babulpur and nearby villages. Kartik was one of those, who had been beaten mercilessly by the police a few days back, when he took away the plough and the bullocks of Dinabandhu Das and his men to prevent them from occupying the land.'

Darga and Mona got up and went straight to the two young men. Looking at them straight into their eyes, Darga said, 'Babu, we did not expect that we will get everything immediately after our party wins the vote, but after all those hard days of rallies and protests, we feel that we are being treated as beggars today, hungry for alms from the party.'

Mona added, 'Even now we have to give attendance in court in the criminal cases filed against us during the labour strike called by the party two years back. We may even be sent to jail for years, if we can't engage an advocate to defend us. We are not alone. Many more sitting there are facing the same plight.'

From the chaos that followed, Hadam could only catch the names Paran and Prankrishno. Some of them must have recalled the killing of Paran, and the failure of the party to get his killers arrested and punished. Suddenly, the heaviness in his chest vanished. Was it due to the after effect of the mahua he had consumed? Or the guilt about Paran? Hadam could not decide.

The young speaker took over from there. 'Comrades! A few months back, our Land Reforms Minister, who is also one of the senior leaders of the party, promised that the peasants of each village would decide on the distribution of land in that village. No legal document or law should come in the way. Now he is saying that this can be done through the government system, that is, through the BDO (Block Development Officer) or JLRO (Junior Land Reforms Officer). The law of the land should be maintained at all costs. Tell me, comrades! On whose side is he? Is he not protecting the *jotdars*?'

Again there was a chorus, this time announcing 'Yes!', and the young man continued, 'Our leader, Comrade Charu Majumdar has declared that there is no other way except the path shown by Lenin, the way taken forward by Stalin, and the torch kept aflame by Mao Tse Tung. Naxalbari has lit up the same fire. All of you spread this fire everywhere by identifying the worst enemy of the people of your locality, and eliminate him if he refuses to reform himself. The people's court has already punished Balai babu, the most crooked *jotdar* of Ranipur. Time has come for another such step.'

Hadam suddenly felt a chill along his spine. What were they talking about? They wanted to kill someone. Who? He didn't have to wait for the answer for long. Subhas took a few steps forward, and said, 'Comrade, each one of the *jotdars* thrives upon their henchmen. They engage them for breaking down the labourers' unity, evict the sharecroppers, and even kill those people who become a threat to the empire that the rich have built upon the skeletons of the poor people. Everyone knows the number one agent of the *jotdars* in Babulpur.'

It was Kartik again, who leapt up from where he was sitting and shouted, 'Heeru... that bastard, mother—'

But this time, he was not alone. A few voices echoed his words, though the men at the back did not stand up. Subhas carried it forward from there. 'The most dangerous among them is Heeru. He had provoked us—Hari, Kanan, and me, to fight, and then sent us to jail at the behest of *jotdars*. He tried to break the strike, and had beaten Kartik and other labourers mercilessly. The police lodged Hari in prison for that. I am sure it was he who killed Paran for a hefty sum given to him by the *jotdars*, and none else. Heeru is the one, who should be removed first.'

An eerie silence followed over the next few seconds, until the bespectacled young man broke into speech again.

'Comrades, it is time for direct action. The enemy of the people will be identified by the court of the people and punished, but we have to be cautious. Let us part today with this resolution. We will meet again soon.'

Hadam was feeling giddy. He hurriedly came out of Budha's hut even without taking a look at the liquor bottles. He came out and sat under the dark shadow of the tamarind tree, and tried to recollect what he had just heard. Someone touched his shoulder from behind. Hadam looked back. Cold sweat broke out from his forehead. Trailokya waved his hand, asking to follow him.

He suddenly remembered that the police had conducted many raids to catch Subhas, dead or alive. Today Subhas had come out from his secret den for the first time. Had Trailokya seen him? A chill went down his spine. Why was Chowkidar Trailokya here? And why did he ask Hadam of all people, to follow him? Moreover, he was wearing a crumpled shirt and a short dhoti, instead of the usual khaki uniform that included a broad belt with the image of three lions embossed on the buckle, the symbol of power given to him by the police and the government.

Trailokya put one hand on Hadam's shoulder, and like a long lost friend, he said endearingly, 'Hadam bhai, why have you come here? Are you here to attend the meeting of these Naxals, who are nothing but anti-social elements? Your son, Comrade Hari, holds a very high rank in the party. Everybody knows that he is very close to Sukumar babu, the District Secretary and the chief of the party. Don't you know that these upstarts, by lecturing here, have broken away from the main party? Their days are numbered.'

Hadam stared at him vacantly for some time. He was taken aback because of the unusual respect shown to him by none other than the chowkidar of the village, the only government representative in the locality, who had been given the seal of the government: those three lions on the buckle of his leather belt that stared at the offenders of law sternly. Moreover, he could not find a single reason to contradict what he had understood from the lecture of the young man. What happened to Paran? Wasn't he working with utmost dedication for the party? He, the most sincere worker of the party, was silenced (killed) by the *jotdars*, only because he had tried to keep the promise the leaders had made before the election. No one bothered to find out why it happened, and how. Now, others would think twice before taking up a fight against the *jotdars*. What happened to the killers? Nothing! No one had been arrested so far. Had a *jotdar* been killed, the police would have arrested all those present in the vicinity, within one kilometre around the spot.

However, Hadam could only say, 'Tailok, I couldn't understand much of what they said. Maybe I have grown too old to understand the present situation. The only thing which is bugging me is why these educated young men have left their college, their families, and their homes in the city, and have come to this godforsaken village to work for the peasants.'

Trailokya had no answer, but he got the reassurance he was seeking, that there was no threat so far as Comrade Hari and his father were concerned. He left Hadam where he was standing and hurried to inform the Circle Inspector waiting a few hundred metres from there, in his jeep, tucked away behind the Ashwatha tree. Hadam got up and slowly moved towards home. He needed to speak to Hari that night itself.

# Babu's Saraswati Puja

Chanchal da was missing from the pandal for quite some time. We managed to fix the tarpaulin cover over the bamboo poles with a lot of difficulty. We collected those poles from our own backyard and the tarpaulin from Gajen babu's godown with the promise to return those intact after Saraswati Puja. If these were damaged due to our inept handling, all of us would be in trouble. I suggested that we should take the help of Monu, who worked in our house on annual contract and lived with us. We could have taken his help at least for digging the holes, for which we need not have paid, but Chanchal da was adamant that everything had to be done by us from scratch. And we had done everything we could have, to live up to his expectations, though without much result on the ground. This was no time for him to go missing.

Just after Kali Puja and Deepavali, Chanchal da announced that this year's Saraswati Puja would be performed out in the open, where everybody could join. After a long discussion, we decided to organize the puja under the banner of Tarun Sangha, the long defunct club of Babulpur. Years back, my father, then part of a young brigade, and his friends had formed the club with many noble objectives like reviving *jatra*—the open air folk theatre, running a night school, playing volleyball, etc., but the enthusiasm evaporated as quickly as it grew after a fiasco about staging the first *jatra*. Grandfather revealed the secret behind the decision to close the club.

The play they had chosen was *Hara Parvati*, a mythological play, so that the elders would support them. It would have been a sacrilege to even think of casting any girl from the village in the female roles, and no young man agreed to play the roles of goddesses Durga, Laxmi, or Saraswati. Bhupen babu was engaged as Motion Master to direct the play and also to arrange professional actresses for the female roles. Yamuna Rani, a professional actress of repute, was appointed for the main role, of Parvati, and two junior actresses, Kamala and Radhika, for two other roles for a hefty amount.

Bhusan babu, handsome, and matriculate, the son of Trailokya babu, was selected for the role of Shiva. In his enthusiasm of being as realistic as possible onstage, he exceeded the motions given to him by the Motion Master even in the rehearsals. The physical proximity of Shiva and Parvati did not go unnoticed. His wife brought the rumor to the notice of his father, and he issued an ultimatum to his son to drop out from the play immediately. A few other actors also fought among each other to win over the other two actresses. No one was sure whether one of them succeeded, or all. The village grapevine was fed with different stories of one or the other being caught red-handed behind a bamboo bush or a hay stack with one of the two actresses.

It was quite natural that there would be frequent late night quarrels in a number of bedrooms in the village, which routinely spilled over to the courtyard in the morning, and reached the banks of Babui River by noon. Finally, the Gram Sabha was convened. Majority of the elders supported Trailokya babu in his tirade against the *jatra*. However, the young club members were determined to stage the play. A compromise was reached, only because a lot of money had already flown down the drain by then. Both the groups agreed to prepone the staging of the play, so that the relationship between the actors and actresses would not get the time to grow to an unmanageable level.

The play was a hit, though the prompters delivered most of the dialogues on time, instead of the actors. The make-up man also did a splendid job. With the help of glittering dresses, he transformed the dark skinned young men into identifiable gods like Vishnu, Brahma, and Indra. And that was the end of the club culture in Babulpur.

We revived the club after decades. It was a rebellion of sort to go for the Baroari Puja, a concept derived from the words 'baro yaar' or twelve friends, who performed a puja together; but the worship of Saraswati, the goddess of learning, outside the enforced sanctity of the family was resisted strongly in Babulpur. The situation became tense when, under the leadership of Chanchal da, we proposed to invite all the school going children of Babulpur, including those from lower caste families and Adivasis to participate in the puja. Fierce debates continued for days. The books carrying the stench of the untouchable Hadi or Dhopa children would be placed before the goddess; children of the lower castes and Adivasis would offer *pushpanjali*, a floral tribute, at the feet of the goddess of learning. All this was unthinkable even a few years back, but now the village had no option left. On one hand, there were their own disobedient children, and on the other, the arrogant kids from these two communities—products of the changed power structure; both were unpredictable. The headman of Babulpur reluctantly decided to keep out of it, saying, 'Times have changed. It was all predicted in the *Bhavishya Puran*, even the impending Shudra Rule in Kaliyuga.' They kept their distance from the entire event.

I divulged the secret to Sarasati the very next day, when we were coming back from school. Initially she was scared, but moments later, she started planning what all she would do, beginning with the sari she would wear and the blouse, bra, and petticoat she would borrow from her Asha mai. I looked at her and felt for the first time that she looked like a full grown young woman, with a well developed body with curves and a tempting rhythmic movement all over.

Our enthusiasm was short-lived. Village elders did not enforce their dictates even though they were livid with anger. However, the Brahman priest of Durga, the reigning deity of Babulpur, came out against it openly. This was nothing but sacrilege for the staunch followers of Manu, who bestowed upon them the privilege of protecting the Hindu way of life. We were also determined to bring about a rebellion of sorts in Babulpur. When we unanimously declared that we wouldn't participate in any puja if these children were not allowed to participate, another interpretation in support was found, and the Brahman finally agreed to be the priest for our puja. One fallout of the entire episode was that Chanchal da and his family were held responsible for all the troubles in the otherwise 'peaceful' Babulpur.

'These Bangals from East Bengal will spoil our children, and why not? They threw out their tradition, their religion in River Padma before they crossed over to this side as refugees.'

'Who knows about what they did there, for which they had to flee like swarms of flies? They used to call the poor Musalman labourers "lere" and lived a luxurious life themselves. Now, in our country wherever you go, you see them everywhere—working in the fish market, vegetable market, chicken and mutton shops, which no Hindu would do even if they have to starve to death. So, it is no wonder that most of them have become communists.'

'Now they want to poison the minds of our young people, so that these foolish village brats follow in their footsteps. Chanchal has deliberately planned to invite the children of those savage Adivasis and Shudras for the Saraswati Puja, who were never even allowed to step inside the gates of our temples, let alone participate in the pujas, and that too in Saraswati Puja, the worship of the goddess of learning. And see! Our children are dancing to his tunes.'

'Times have changed, dada. This is Kali Yuga; now you have to serve those people, who had begged for a handful of rice from you yesterday. *Kalki Puran* cannot be wrong. The end of this world is not very far. The outsiders will now decide how you have to live in your society, isn't it? The wise thing will be to accept the destiny and wait for your time.'

Chanchal's family moved out from East Bengal, from the communal riot, the genocide, the dance of the goddess of death, just before the Partition of Bengal and Independence of India. 'East Pakistan' was what it was called thereafter. Communal riots engulfed villages and towns, both in the west and the east. Hindus butchered Musalmans in West Bengal and Musalmans killed Hindus in East Bengal; just the recurrence of what happened in East Punjab and West Punjab in the north. A blood soaked sun brought independence to India and Pakistan on 15 August 1947. On that morning, Mohan babu,

Chanchal's father, was frantically searching for a roof with four walls for his mother and young wife instead of celebrating independence. He was the only adult male in the family who survived the great exodus. His father and uncle perished in the fire, which engulfed their ancestral house, after they refused to leave, hoping that the age-old relationship would protect them. While fleeing from their village in Barishal, they had to leave behind everything the family possessed. At last, along with the other unfortunate millions, they were given a shed to lie down in one of the makeshift tents put up for them, and allowed them to die in hundreds due to starvation and Cholera. Even when they were relocated, they were packed in a truck and offloaded at some godforsaken place like this abandoned marshland called Kalaboni in Narayanpur. They got the name 'refugee', the term for displaced and helpless people who fled from their homeland and took refuge in an alien land.

The people of Babulpur, like the others from this part of Bengal, were called Ghoti, maybe due to the perception that they are a closed society like the narrow necked brass pots of the same generic name. True to the term, they were convinced that these Bangals deserted not only their ethics, but also every pretence of gentlemanly behaviour the day they left their homeland, and that now they had no qualms about even bartering their soul in exchange for a few currency notes. They believed that these people were destroying the age old traditions and values, which had still survived in this part of Bengal. It would be naïve to think that these comments did not reach those for whom they were intended, but Chanchal da or his family did not react, or at least, we did not hear anything from them.

We were quite taken aback when Hari came to meet us along with Sarasati and two-three boys and girls in the evening before the day of the puja. They brought bananas, berries, and papayas as their offerings for the goddess. Each of them also contributed a little cash as the offering for the priest, a mandatory tradition as per the scriptures for their role as mediator between the gods or goddesses and the devotees.

Hari sat down with us and, in his inimitable style, said, 'Babu, I don't know what you people thought, when you decided to organize a Baroari Puja and invited these children also. You know, we Adivasis also celebrate the fortnight of ascending moon in the month of Magha. Let me sing a song:

The soft, chilly Magha wind
Swept through Daahi, Dungri and bushes
It is time for night long song and dance
With pot full *handiya* brewed for weeks...'

His full-throated voice filled the air through the evening. The celebration of the onset of spring in gay abandon was not unknown to us. Suddenly, my eyes fell on Sarasati. I was caught, as she was keeping an eye on me. She smiled mischievously, but for Hari, it was time for some serious considerations. There was concern in his tone, when he said,

'Whatever you people might have thought before organizing this puja, for me, it is a very good beginning. The Adivasis of Singbhum are now selling the dream of Jharkhand, a state exclusively for Adivasis, among our people, particularly the younger generation. They are exhorting the people to sharpen their arrows and *tangis* to fight for a homeland of Adivasis and Adivasis alone. They take the names of Adivasi heroes like Captain Jaipal Singh, Surjo Singh Besra, and others. Our boys are confused. They are not sure whether their small villages in the outskirts of Babulpur can become a part of Jharkhand, the homeland of Adivasis. They identify themselves with the Adivasis of Jhargram, Purulia, and Singbhum because, even after three generations, the isolation of Adivasis here is also a fact of their lives. This kind of interaction among the young people of both the communities is the only way to avert the crisis. Let Ma Saraswati give us some sanity, so that we can live in harmony.'

Hari left with others with the promise that everyone from their community will join us tomorrow. Chanchal da sneered after they left, 'See, this is the kind of leaders that the Communist Party brews. These illiterate communists, who have not even read the Manifesto, are responsible for the decline of Marxism everywhere.'

We dug holes in the ground ourselves for the first time in life with a lot of enthusiasm to fix the bamboo poles. All of us got our palms bruised and skin abraded in our effort to dig holes with iron rods. Now, the colourful saris we had collected were to be hung to cover the bamboo poles under the direction of Kajol didi. Then we were to paste colourful paper flowers and paper chains designed by Chanchal da, to give the pandal a rainbow look around the all-white idol of Goddess Saraswati placed in the centre with her veena and swan. Sulekha and Srilekha, the two sisters of Chanchal da, were waiting for Kajol didi to help them to put the pleats on the saris.

We fanned out to different directions to trace Chanchal da, as he was to guide us at this crucial juncture. It was already late in the evening and it was getting dark fast. We had only a few lanterns, definitely not enough to work with thread, needle, and scissors. Where did he disappear suddenly? Within a few minutes, Shombhu came back running from the backside of the pandal and fell down on the mat in a very dramatic fashion. He burst out with laughter and started rolling on the mat, with his eyes sparkling in the twilight. It was evident from his face that he was going to reveal some secret very soon. We gathered around him in anticipation. After a few seconds, he waved to us to come still closer, and whispered, 'Chanchal da and Kajol didi...' and then gestured with his lips, unmistakably resembling a passionate kiss. All of us were dumb struck for a moment and clamoured to hear more from him. What he had just described seemed to have been drawn straight out of a filmy romantic scene. Kajol didi looked like Sharmila Tagore in 'An Evening in Paris', a film which we had heard about, but didn't have the permission to watch. But more pressing things were waiting; so we left it there, and decided to wait for Chanchal da.

He appeared on the scene sooner than expected and Kajol didi took another few minutes. Chanchal da was very cool, but her eyes wore a pink hue and the cheeks crimson. Our eyes searched every single limb of her body to find any trace of what had taken place during the last few minutes. She must have noticed it, and wore a sullen face. But without any sign of guilt on his face, Chanchal da looked around and thumped on our backs in an obvious attempt to explain his absence, 'Very good! You have done a fantastic job. No labourer could have done this. Now, Kajol, get on with your work. Hang the saris from the string carefully, so that the bamboos are covered. After that, boys! Paste the paper flowers and paper chains and give the finishing touch to the pandal.' Kajol didi did not utter a word during the entire evening and left abruptly after her work was over.

While going back home at almost midnight, Shombhu described to me with graphic details of what he had seen:

'Chanchal da hugged Kajol didi tightly and kissed her repeatedly. His hands were fondling her breasts with the blouse unbuttoned, as if he was squeezing an orange. It was so...beautiful! Amal re! I can't describe...'

Shombhu was wiser than me in these matters and taught me the basics of sex. He claimed to have had several intercourses with their maid, a widow, much older than him, in the bamboo grove behind his house, till she eloped with the flutist of a *jatra* company. I didn't believe him, because I had heard his many other fantasies in all these years. As he was going into more details, I realized that something was stirring inside me; a blind lust overpowered me, urging me to penetrate the veil of secrecy. Shombhu must have understood my state of mind. He took my hand in his and pulled it towards his groin. I could feel his hardened penis. With the other hand he touched mine. In the very next moment, he pushed me aside against the wall nearby, pulled my half-pants down, and started fondling my penis slowly. After a few seconds, he placed my own hand there and said, 'Do it yourself.' Shombhu and I ejaculated almost together and leaned on the nearest tree, till I recovered from the tumultuous experience to be able to walk. My abdomen and groin hurt with an unknown pleasure and pain. A strange feeling of guilt seeped in when I remembered about the puja the next day.

From the day Chanchal da's family came to our village and started living here permanently, he became our hero. He was already a graduate; he was the star centre forward of his college, and now our coach and mentor. He could sing both Hindi and Bangla songs well. All of us knew for sure and others in the village suspected that he and Kajol didi were having an affair. Almost every evening they were seen together, sometimes sitting on the Babui Bridge, sometimes walking along the railway line, engrossed in conversation. But this was the first time that they had been seen in a compromising position. I was afraid. Kajol didi's father, Kalipada Chakraborty, was the priest of the Shitala temple, and the entire village used to look up to him in matters spiritual. He and his sons were known for their aggressive Brahman ego. If they came to know about this relationship, they would definitely teach this son of Bangal non-Brahman a lesson, and would not spare his family, either.

Chanchal da was the eldest among the three sons and two daughters of Mohan babu, an elderly clerk in the BDO office. He had taken the dilapidated house of Rajen Maity on rent, which Rajen babu had abandoned after constructing a new one. His intention was to convert it into a warehouse for his bamboo business, but he gave it on rent and also utilized the open space in the front for stacking bamboos. This was the first time someone had rented a house in Babulpur. Within a few days of his shifting, everyone in the village realized that Mohan babu's meagre salary was not enough to run his family smoothly. That's why he came to this village and rented a house at a much cheaper rate than Narayanpur. He used to go to Narayanpur by cycle to attend office. He would go to Rajen babu's shop late in the evening to buy rice, mustard oil, dal, and other groceries. From the very first day the agreement was that he would pay in the first week of every month after he got his salary. Chanchal da was unemployed. He helped his father as much as he could from the small amount he earned from his tuitions after paying for his brother's—Sajal's education; but his two sisters, Sulekha and Srilekha, dropped out of school after shifting to Babulpur.

Mohan babu maintained a distance from everybody, be it his family, or his neighbours. He talked in a low voice, walked with measured steps, and maintained a strict routine. We, the children who used to take tuitions from Chanchal da, always found him reading some book or the other, and his mother, whom we called Masima, compensated with her love and affection for all of us. We had free access even to her kitchen and shared whatever she prepared. We regularly got a treat of exquisite *pithe* and *payas* prepared with Gobindobhog rice and milk, be it the occasion of Paus Sankranti, Vijaya Dashami, or the birthdays of her children. We openly admitted that only Masima could prepare such authentic delicacies, much to the torment of our mothers, grandmothers, and aunts, as they lamented that these Bangals were responsible for spoiling their children by better appeasing their tastebuds.

I got up early next morning and ran towards the pandal without even a wrapper, despite the chilly Magha winds. The pandal shined there in its colourful get-up in contrast to the hazy surroundings. Chanchal da must have worked the whole night to give it the final touch. As I got closer I saw no one except the idol of Goddess Saraswati with her veena and swan, dressed in all white splendours. Even Kajol didi had not turned up. She was supposed to come early and arrange everything for the puja.

When I entered the pandal, my eyes got glued on the back of a girl sitting behind the idol with her double pleated hair swinging on the red blouse. The neck-line and shoulder seemed familiar to me. I have watched her from the back many a time. The boys most often managed to walk behind the group of girls on their way to school. I have been around whenever she told me that she will be going to the Thursday Haat for the cock-fight, or when she joined the community dance during their *parab* under the soft glow of full moon. But today she looked so different in a white sari and red blouse that I was feeling shaky to go near her. She looked like a beautiful grown up woman, with the unmistakable curve of her body, hiding her small but firm breasts.

She must have felt the heat of my lusty eyes. I was caught unaware, when she suddenly turned towards me. With her face still moist after a morning bath, well-oiled combed hair, and kohl rimmed eyes, Sarasati looked like a goddess. She was arranging books for keeping those in front of the idol. A brass plate was kept in front of her with a few bananas, oranges, flowers, and a piece of red cloth arranged neatly. She smiled sheepishly, when she looked up and saw me staring at her, and her face changed colour, as if she, with her feminine instinct, could see through my thoughts, and said,

'Asha mai made me wear all this. She also asked me to take these offerings and my books. One should not come empty-handed to Ma Saraswati, nah?'

Her mysterious and enchanting eyes coaxed me to break free. I wanted to be with her, away from the pandal for a few minutes, like Chanchal da with Kajol didi. Perhaps she would have come with me had I asked her, but I was afraid that Sarasati would turn into Goddess Durga, the furious destroyer of demons, if I made any attempt to follow in the footsteps of Chanchal da. Ma Saraswati, the goddess of learning, can see everything with all pervasive eyes. She was going to punish me for what I had done last night. The punishment would be doubled if I committed another sin today. I required her blessings the most for the upcoming board examinations. So I did the next best thing; I sat down near her, touched her fingers softly, and said, 'Sarasati, you look so sweet in a sari, I cannot take my eyes off you. Why don't you wear one often?'

Sarasati blushed. Holding my left palm, she pressed it so hard that I almost cried out in agony. This Adivasi girl is so strong! She moved away from me a little, and whispered, 'I know what I am; a Santhal girl, black and ugly. I don't know why you invited us from the Adivasi Para for this puja. Our people were in dilemma. Some of them, in fact, suspected foul play. It is Daddu, who told me to participate in the puja, because the invitation came from you, the grandson of Santosh Pradhan. You know what else he said? You are as brave as your grandfather. I shall always remember how you have taken care of me from the day I joined your school.You helped me in building my confidence to face the problems as an Adivasi. It is the respect you have given us by inviting us to participate in the puja despite so much resistance from your own people, for which I have decided to be with you, come what may. My father and mother died long back. Now, my Baap is both father and mother to me. He is an active member of the party that has taken away your land, your position, and has brought you people down to the level of the common men. Many people will be very happy to see him eliminated as quickly as possible. Despite all this, why are you helping us?'

I was completely bowled out by her indirect admission of love. It was with great difficulty that I suppressed an irresistible desire to hug her. I stammered, but managed to speak out, 'Sarasati, I love you as you are. I don't know what my father or grandfather did, or for that matter, your father and grandfather. Now the party is out of power. The equations have changed, but I am with you and will remain so. Chanchal da often says that one has to make conscious efforts to erase the class consciousness to become a true revolutionary; the ultimate goal of the revolution is to achieve a classless society, where we all will be equal.'

Sarasati closed her eyes for a moment, and said, 'I don't understand all these complicated lectures, but now I want to tell you something that you may not like. You should be careful. People suspect that Chanchal dada is one of those people, who were involved in the murder of Balai babu. A few days back, you went with him to attend a meeting in Kol Para, where Subhas and his friends were also present. He has already told people that he has recruited you in their party; you, the son of Naren babu, are a prized possession for their party. Not many people know this till now. But, it will spread out faster than you can imagine, and you will be in trouble.'

I was stunned. A few days back, Chanchal da had asked me to accompany him in the evening, without disclosing the destination or purpose. We went to a small village, which had a few small huts surrounded by big trees and thorny bushes. I could not recognize even one of the twenty-odd people who had assembled there. However, I could hear the whispers going around among the people as we walked past them towards the front. Three young men sat there facing others; they distinctly belonged to a class of people different from us. Their demeanor reflected the educated and urban stamp. One of them was in the midst of his lecture—

'...Our leader and guide, Comrade Charu Majumdar, has chalked out the path of revolution in his article "A Few Words about Guerilla Actions", recently published in our magazine, *Liberation*. He has said, "Guerilla Units will be formed clandestinely. It should be kept secret not only from our supporters, but even from those party units, which have not adopted themselves to the concept of armed uprising and discipline of a revolutionary party. These underground secret units shall eliminate big landlords through covert operations and guerilla action. The aim is to capture power in rural areas; declare one village at a time as a liberated zone after some of the landlords are killed, and the rest are forced to leave the village in fear. And then, under the supervision of a revolutionary committee, land reform will be taken up as part of exercising power of the peoples' state."'

'Last year we formed the Bengal Bihar Orissa Border Regional Committee (BBOBRC), the committee for the adjoining regions of the three states. A few months back, precisely on 27 September, we launched our first successful action. You must have heard about the actions in Debra. The peasants themselves pronounced the verdict to eliminate the most notorious *jotdar* of the area. In the village, Kusum Gram, near Debra, lived the richest landlord of the district with a landholding of 2000 bighas. He compelled every farm labourer who came to him for *dadan* to work for a few days in his field as *begaar* (for free). To punish the errant peasants, he maintained a group of *paiks*, who were employed to maim or even kill those who protested or to burn their huts, whenever they wanted. The police toed his line, because he paid them a lot of money. He had connections right up to the top. When the peasants of Debra identified him as their worst enemy and the people's court announced capital punishment to him, he was eliminated by the action squad of peasants led by this young man, Comrade Amrit.'

The young man, who raised his hands, was a bespectacled slim young fellow. From his frail body he didn't look even remotely capable of facing even a local goonda, let alone kill such a powerful landlord; but a grim determination in his narrow eyes, just above the protruding emaciated cheek bones, betrayed an uncanny power within him. He remained silent despite several 'zindabad'-s being added to his name in the slogans raised by everyone in the room.

The elderly man continued. A few names, familiar to all by now, in this district at least, were dropped too often. The names of Santosh Rana, Jangal Santhal, and Charu Majumdar were uttered with immense awe, like a Hindu devotee chanting the holy names of their 33 crore deities. I still remember that he narrated many incidents of uprising by the peasants throughout India and mentioned about the people killed in those places. During that hour or so, only once one of those suave young men asked me my name. Chanchal da answered before I could say anything, 'He is the grandson of Santosh Pradhan, a very rich and powerful landlord of this village. But this boy is different; a sincere friend of the poor Adivasis, who also love him a lot. He helps me in organizing meetings and accompanies me everywhere.' I felt very embarrassed, and at the same time, nervous.

How Sarasati came to know about that evening was still troubling me. The implication of the visit she was talking about was frightening. I said, 'Sarasati, believe me, I went there only because Chanchal da asked me to go with him, but how do you know about all this?'

Sarasati smiled and said, 'Some people came that very night and told Baap everything. The moment I heard your name, I stood behind the door to understand what is happening. Baap told them not to discuss this anywhere else. Later, when I asked, he said, "They think that by assassinating a *jotdar* or his henchmen through guerilla action, they will gain the sympathy of the peasants. Yes! They will gain their sympathy, but they will also be afraid, and friendship cannot grow where fear exists. Such action can never unite the peasants for the long drawn struggle against the system, which is required to change the social order. The commitment behind such individual killings is always limited to one individual member of the action squad and an inactive mass of peasants, who follow them more out of fear rather than their belief in Marxism. In such a situation, armed revolution is a day dream of a few misguided city-bred young bhadraloks. And I am also sure of one thing: Babu, being Naren's son, has been identified, and it will not remain a secret. Warn him to be careful in the future, and come out of this trap."'

I pulled her towards me in a moment of frenzy and hugged her tightly. Sarasati brought both her hands between us, pushed me away from her, laughed silently, and said, 'Ma Saraswati is looking at us. Behave yourself! Bhai is also playing outside. He may come down any moment.' I felt very embarrassed and left in a huff.

The rituals of worship went on smoothly. The priest recited Sanskrit slokas from a thin book, understood by nobody, and perhaps, not even by him. At the end of the puja, we, the devotees, recited a set of mantras and offered flowers. Sarasati joined the prayer with us, but they stood in a separate row. They made sincere efforts to repeat the slokas recited by the priest. Their voice was louder than us. At the end of it all, a smile of contentment radiated on our faces, the happiness of breaking the shackles, standing on the same pedestal with children from the other side of Babui River. Sarasati must have remembered her father fighting for his right to embrace Christianity and his tragic death after he was ex-communicated from their community. She was firm in her resolve to exercise her right to select the path she wanted to pursue and she was sure that had Joba been alive, she would have been the happiest person to see her today.

# Babu in Trouble

The euphoria of the success of the first community puja in Babulpur did not last long, at least for me. After a few days, on one foggy morning, Heeru's dead body was found on a barren paddy field at the outskirts of Kamar Para; his belly neatly cut from one side to another and his bluish intestine was out in the open, protruding out of the thick fatty layer of the belly. It was an eerie silence that reigned all around Babulpur for the first few hours. No one came out of their house on either side of Babui River, as if they could not even trust their neighbours.

Heeru's wife managed to put a soiled dhoti upon his body to ward off the flies and insects. She was sitting there all alone and crying. Her children roamed around listlessly. A few people were loitering and keeping watch from a distance. They were perhaps waiting for the police to arrive. The only thing no one touched were a few newspaper pages on which 'Naxalbari Zindabad', 'Mao Tse Tung jug jug jeo' were written in red ink. The dreaded members of his group and Heeru's constant companions were nowhere to be seen.

After the warm sunshine removed the fog, Prankrishno reached the spot with his young friends, followed by the trusted men of Heeru.

It was clear from their ashen faces and terrified eyes that they were shaken to the core by the brutal killing. Almost at the same time, a jeep load of police also arrived from Narayanpur. Slowly, the place was crammed with people from Babulpur, surrounding villages, and curious onlookers from outside. The noise of incessant talking among the mob often degenerated into heated discussions and reached the level of the weekly market of Babulpur. 'Shut up!'—one shout by Gopal Daroga and there was pin drop silence. He was in a nasty mood. Many people in the front row also received nasty blows with his baton, after which they beat a hasty retreat from the dead body, but others continued to surge ahead and get beaten. Someone brought a chair and placed it under the banyan tree. A photographer was taking shots, after which the police would wrap the body and take it away. Daroga babu took his seat and called Gunu, Heeru's wife for her preliminary statement.

Heeru had come back rather early the last evening, with a bottle of country liquor and fried chickpeas. He consumed half a bottle and asked for food. He was in a foul mood, and therefore, the routine beating of Gunu over the quality of cooking was harder than usual. Gunu finished the left overs and went to bed. Heeru was smoking a biri after dinner. Then he went out to relieve himself. She was waiting for him for the finale of the day, a round of fuck, if he was in the mood for that, when she heard a voice. She could understand a few words, 'Heeru bhai! Heeru bhai!' After that, it was only the humming of the cricket.

Daroga babu intervened, 'Was that voice of a bhadralok or like someone of your community?'

Gunu remained silent for a while, and then said, 'To me it sounded like that of an Adivasi, like…like that of Paran!'

'Bullshit! How could you say it was Paran's voice? Can ghosts speak?' thundered the daroga. 'How did you discover the body? Where?'

She sobbed. Clearing her throat, she said, 'When he did not come back even after a long time, I was afraid. But then, he often used to go out late in the night without disclosing anything. So I didn't go out in search of him. After sometime I fell asleep. Palu and Kalu, our neighbours woke me up early in the morning and told me about this. He was lying here only. I have been requesting him to be careful since long, but he didn't care. Now, see, where he has left me and my children. Oh God! What—'

Gopal Daroga impatiently waved at her to stop. He wrapped up the inquest with a few questions to Kalu and Palu. The jeep belched out black smoke and Daroga babu left for Narayanpur with the dead body and the posters written in red ink on old news papers.

And that was where things took a wrong turn for me.

Gopal babu came back in the evening by the same jeep. Based on the concrete evidence of Naxal involvement available in those posters, he straightaway handcuffed Chanchal da and bundled him into the jeep. The combing operation to nab Subhas was so intense that the entire Kol Para was turned upside down. No one was spared, not even the women, children, and the old. A few male members of Kol Para were picked up and thrashed black and blue. The police warned everyone around that unless Subhas surrendered, they would come again with more force, and maybe even with the COBRA (Commando Battallion for Resolute Action).

Taking a clue from the statement given by some of those arrested, an armed police party led by Gopal Daroga himself came to my house the next day. The first question he asked Baba (father) was, 'Do you know what your son is up to? He has joined the Naxals. He even attended their meetings. We have information that he is very close to Chanchal Sarkar. I want to ask him a few questions. Call him, here!'

Baba was dumbstruck and could not answer for few seconds. After he gathered his wits, he told him what any other father would say, 'He is a child. He does not know what he has been doing. It must be his teacher, Chanchal, who has misled him into this. I will see to it that he does not do this again.'

Gopal babu was a seasoned police officer with years of experience. He sternly asked my father to call me. When Baba came inside, it was all chaos. I took shelter in a corner. My legs were trembling uncontrollably. Ma was weeping loudly. Satyabhama, my grandmother, was so agitated that she yelled at Baba for following the daroga's orders. She then barged into the bedroom and irreverently jolted awake Santosh, my grandfather, who was in his routine daytime slumber.

Baba then dragged me to the front room where the daroga was sitting. I could hear my heart beat and feel the throb at the nape of my neck as I stood before him. The first question he asked was in a cold voice, '*Babajibon*, is it true that you went to Kol Para with Chanchal?'

I could not even utter a word in reply. He asked again, 'Who all were there? Any outsider? Do you remember any name?'

I could feel the impending roughness of his palms on my cheeks without even him touching me. He suddenly took my face in vice, as if within the grip of his fingers, turned it towards him, and said in a cold voice, 'A man has been killed! His belly was slit by a knife. This has happened for the first time in Narayanpur. This kind of killing has come from the city, Kolkata; someone from there. You were there in the meeting. Who is the killer? Tell me, who is it?'

I distinctly remembered the face of Comrade Amrit and the name as well, but like a stubborn mule, I remained silent till I could bear the pain. At last I cried out in pain, and said sobbing, 'I don't know. There were 10–15 people, but I have never seen any of them before.'

Gopal Daroga tightened his grip and pulled me towards himself. His big red eyes were upon my face. He was about to ask me something tougher, but before he could utter even the first word, Grandfather came out from nowhere. He caught hold of his hand, and said coldly, 'Leave him, Daroga babu. You are knocking at the wrong door. There have been many a murder case in Narayanpur during the past one year; many more will be committed in the next few months. You cannot hold a 14-year-old boy responsible for all such murders, particularly when a known hoodlum of the area has been killed. And even if he is guilty, he has to be tried in a juvenile court. This type of investigation will not help you in your career.'

The daroga was well aware of the reputation of the Pradhan family. We had been staunch supporters of Congress from the days of the Quit India Movement. Santosh and Baidyanath were in the forefront of the fight against the British in this area, under the leadership of Deben Das. They were arrested and were in jail for sometime. Gopal Daroga's jaws stiffened, but he released me and said, 'Santosh babu, the times have changed and so has the profiles of the killers. You never know who would kill whom and why. I could have extracted my information today, but since he is your grandson, I am sparing him for the time being. I don't know why, even Hari Santhal, the President of Krishak Sabha, has denied any involvement of this boy with the Naxals of the area, though many others have mentioned it. Isn't it strange? Whatever it is, I am leaving now, but I shall advise you to be careful in the future. If I come again, I shall not go back empty-handed.'

It was all darkness in Chanchal da's house when I entered. Sulekha and Srilekha were sitting in the verandah, huddled together. Mohan babu was not there at his table and neither were his books. Everything in their possession had been torn apart by the police and thrown out in the verandah: clothes, books, utensils, and even rice, dal, and vegetables. Masima was sitting in the kitchen before the cold chullah, doing nothing. I stood there silently for some time. At last, when Masima noticed me, she said, 'Chanchal is not here, baba. Why have you come here? You will be in trouble. Now, I hear that he is a leader of the Naxals; he is a murderer; he is fighting against the government. They want to turn the world upside down. Make the poor people rich. He cared about the labourers and peasants, but never about us. Just see! He has left us nowhere today.'

I had no answer. I saw what I thought I would. Sulekha rescued me from that awkward situation. She pulled me by my hand, took me to the other end of the house. In semi-darkness, she pressed me against the wall with her body and whispered, 'Don't mind. She has gone mad. Baba is running around to borrow some money to engage an advocate and secure bail for Dada. We don't even have rice to eat this evening. Gajen babu refused to give any grocery unless we pay. Baba has gone out to find out if he can get some advance from his office, or pawn whatever little gold is left with Ma, and borrow from people known to him. But I know, nobody will give anything for the family of a Naxal. Can you do something for us? Get some rice for us to eat this evening and 10-15 rupees to buy dal and vegetables. Can't you do this much for me?' She kissed my lips, rubbed hers on my cheek, led my hands to her breasts, and pressed; she was panting. Her warm breath singed my face. Cold sweat broke out from my forehead. I could feel her desperation to save her loved ones from starvation. But why did she have to approach me in this manner?

Suddenly, I felt a pain in my chest. I decided to take a risk and tell everything to my grandmother. Only Satyabhama had the courage to help them at this point. I wriggled out of her hug, pulled my hands out from her grip, and ran away into the darkness.

# Babu in College

The classroom seemed very unfamiliar to me, not at all like those with attached desk and bench sets in my school. This room had around 40 sets of tables and chairs neatly arranged, facing a wooden dais with a pair of table and chair upon it. Girls, comprising almost half of the students in the class, occupied the seats in a haphazard manner sharing the desks with boys. In our school, girls used to sit separately; they would come in groups behind the teacher and leave the class with him.

I might have taken a few seconds at the doorstep to take a look at the faces with whom I would spend the next three years as a student of English Honours and to prepare myself for an unknown world. However, I was brought back to reality with a thud when a rude voice directed at me, rung in my ears, 'Oy *gaandu*! Why are you standing there? Come inside or get lost!' Some of the thirty-odd students burst out in derisive laughter; some of the girls also joined them. I decided to take a seat at the back and moved towards that, but someone pulled my shirt that I had worn loosely, without tucking. Startled, I looked back, but everyone was looking straight. Another fit of laughter; my body stiffened a bit. I turned left and took the chair next to the girl, who, I presumed, had pulled my shirt. I looked at her, a rather plump girl, with a sharp nose and shining thin rimmed spectacles, wearing a yellow polka dot kameez and black salwar. She was trying to hide her smile by putting her hand over her lips, but as soon as I took my seat, she became stiff and moved aside as if trying to avoid any physical contact with me.

Again someone shouted from the back, '*Abé ullu*, why have you parked your bullock cart there? It is for bikes, cars, and smarter guys. Come down to the place earmarked for you among the back benches.' I could feel the anger swelling within me from the throbbing in my temple. I didn't look back and got busy fiddling with my bag. Many more comments flew out from all directions:

'Which village are you from?'

'He is suffering from potato syndrome and requires a sound thrashing to get rid of that.'

'His baap must be a *jotdar*. But this is Contai College. Many of them have come here before and have vanished without a trace.'

The moment I made a move to stand up, there was a tap on my right leg. The girl in polka dot kameez was looking straight ahead, but there was a frown on her face. I looked back. It was a small group of four or five boys sitting in a huddle in the last row, who were passing those remarks. A few amused faces around them enjoyed the fun. Obviously, they were local boys who knew each other. They would have continued with their jibes, but for the dramatic entry of the professor, a man in his late thirties or early forties and very impressively dressed in a trendy shirt, bell-bottom trousers, and pointed shining shoes. With a clean shaven face, he looked much younger than his age. Standing ramrod straight at the edge of the dais, he started in a dramatic manner,

'My dear friends, welcome to the fascinating world of English literature. Let me introduce myself. I am Shantanu Sarcar. My students call me SS; shortly, you will too...'

A murmur went around the class. I could catch one or two familiar words, 'He is a staunch CPM supporter...from Kalna in Bardhaman... a student of Narendrapur Ramakrishna Mission...' But he ignored the noise and continued.

'I am the faculty in-charge for your batch. You can come to me for any problem that you might face in this class or outside, in the college. Firstly, let me make it clear from the beginning that I won't speak in Bangla with you, and I will not accept any language other than English to be spoken to, in this class. If you want to succeed, you have to think in English, dream in English, let alone speak in English. Initially, there will be mistakes, but you must carry on. Gradually, you will learn the tricks. Secondly, before you introduce yourself, I must make it clear that I won't tolerate any indiscipline. Whoever tries to do it, will be simply thrown out of the class room. I don't care which federation or parishad you belong to, you have to maintain discipline in my class. Now, tell me your name, your school, and your stream, starting from the first row, right.'

I tried to remember each name and relate the face of each student. Only one of them impressed me: Barid, a frail young man in dhoti and full sleeve shirt, a rank holder in board examination. The other one was the girl by my side. Her turn came before mine. She was Sudipta, from the local Brahmo Girls School, the oldest and best known girls' school in the district, where rich parents from all corners of the district aspired to send their girls for education, but this time, there was a cat call—'Moyna! Moyna!' It must be her nickname, which got divulged somehow, but she didn't care. After she finished, SS suddenly moved towards the back of the class. It was my turn. But I was so startled that half of my name remained hanging from my lips. SS commanded one of the last benchers sternly, 'Stand up!' He didn't look up. After a few seconds of pin-drop silence, SS hauled him up by the collar of his shirt, pulled him out of his seat, and pushed him towards the door. Ignoring the feeble protests from his friends, SS pushed the boy out of the classroom and came back to his desk dusting his hands, as if he had touched something dusty.

Within a few minutes, even before the introductions were over, some students barged into the class, shouting, 'Chhatra Parishad Jindabad!'... 'CPM agent Shantanu Sarkar, college chhoro!'

It was obvious from their gestures that they were senior students. A few of them could be even outsiders. They stood around SS and started shouting, 'How can you throw a bonafide student of the college out of the class? You have to answer; we will not allow you to take the class until you apologize and take him back.'

SS calmly said, 'He misbehaved with a girl in the clas; I won't allow it. He has to apologize to this girl. And I shall not go out of the class! Do whatever you like.'

One of the newcomers leapt up on the dais and tried to push him. The entire class watched the scuffle helplessly. Suddenly, Sudipta pushed me aside and ran towards the group shouting, 'Stop this nonsense! Don't touch him! This boy was abusing me. Do you people support him? Then, I have to tell this to the students. Let them decide.'

Her outburst was so unexpected that those, who were shouting since they had entered the class room, stood dumb struck for a while, wherever they were. Sudipta pushed one of them and stood on the right hand side of SS. Something inside me compelled me to stand up and move out of my chair. As I got up and started moving towards them, some of the other students in the class also gathered courage and joined me. One of the seniors looked at Sudipta, SS, and then at us. He told his companions in a muffled voice, 'Leave it! We have to ask Jeetu about the details of the incident. Then we will decide what to do with this professor.' After they left, everything went on smoothly for the day.

I could not secure first division in the higher secondary examination and failed to secure a place in the merit list for admission to a medical college. I decided to go back to my first love, English, and applied for English Honours in Contai PK College. Father was furious. He wanted me to drop that year and again try for a seat in the medical college next year. I kept mum till I got the confirmation that I had been selected for English Honours. When I announced my decision, I was firmly told that henceforth I would have to manage my own affairs. My mother and grandparents were very happy that I would be nearer to home and would be able to come home frequently. So I didn't have to worry about my monthly allowance.

After running around for a few days, I could manage a room to share in Bani Bhavan Mess. A group of students rented a two storied building at Karkuli having eight rooms altogether on two floors.

Seniors occupied the better rooms on the first floor with ample light and ventilation. We, the students of first year, were allotted two side rooms on the ground floor, with the condition that we would be promoted to the first floor after the final examinations of third year students by next June or July. By that time, we would be in the second year and fresh students would take our place.

It was an entirely different kind of life for me from my school days. My routine now was to go out for a cup of tea and 'lero' biscuit from Masi's shop early in the morning; go through the books and notes for an hour, and then rush to the back side of the building to be in queue for one of the two makeshift enclosures used as bathrooms. We were compelled to gulp down half-cooked rice with watery lentil and a small piece of fish in red hot curry. Then we ran for our lives to reach college in time to mark attendance for the day.

The walls in the college campus were plastered with posters of Chhatra Parishad (Students' Federation), DSO, and other student fronts of political parties. Each group of students shouted different slogans at the same time and same place, while none of them was audible. They confronted each other and fought pitched battles with bare hands most of the time, but occasionally, sticks would come out of nowhere, and that would be interspersed with stone pelting. Most of the first year students kept themselves away out of fear. Among us in the English Honours class only Sudipta was an active SFI worker. She was even nominated as their candidate from the first year.

My otherwise peaceful world of Shelly, Keats, and Byron turned upside down very soon. At about midnight on a Saturday, somebody pulled the bed sheet away from over me, shook me awake, and whispered my name; it was an unknown face. He signalled me to follow him and left the room in a hurry. Gour da, from third year BSc., remained there to take us, the first years', along. We went out on the road, rubbing our sleepy eyes, and walked silently for a few minutes, before he broke the silence, and said, 'We are going for a pocket meeting of the Naxals. Just sit there and listen patiently. Don't say anything if you want to avoid trouble. We will meet tomorrow in college at the backside of the science building during lunch break. There I shall explain everything.'

Quietly, we walked down a narrow lane from the main road connecting Kanthi with Kharagpur, took a bylane, crossed a pond, and entered a small house, which had no sign of life cognizable from the outside. Gour da knocked gently. Someone peeped through the window to make sure who we were and then opened the door just enough to let in, one at a time. In the dim light of a single candle, I saw about 20 people huddled in a small room. One man sat there leaning on the wall; the only candle was kept in front of him. Though he was a very well built and dark complexioned man with a handlebar moustache, his eyes were almost invisible beyond his prominent cheek bones. He was wearing a khaki shirt that hung loosely on his body, over a pair of white pajamas, which had become almost yellow. One of the two older men broke the silence and said,

'Comrades, we have asked all of you to come here at this time of night, because this is a special day for us, the soldiers of the people's war in Kanthi. Comrade Santosh Rana is here today with us. He does not need any introduction. He is the leader of the peasant uprising in Gopiballavpur and Debra. Though he has travelled throughout the day and attended a number of meetings in Narayangarh, Belda, Egra, and Mohanpur, he has agreed to address us for a short while. The fire raging throughout Bengal, Bihar, and Andhra is going to burn down the feudal state governments and its anti-people machinery very soon. A new dawn is about to herald. If we don't prepare ourselves for the fight, we will lag behind. Let us hear him and rededicate ourselves to bring in the revolution.'

The black complexioned man with a handlebar moustache opened his eyes, straightened himself leaving the support of the wall, and looked straight towards us. When his eyes turned towards me, I felt a shiver inside my belly and goosebumps all over my body. Those two small eyes seemed to be disrobing me in front of everybody. I remembered a night in Babulpur, when someone had mentioned his name in connection with the execution of the biggest landlord of Debra by Naxals. The moment he started his address, his husky voice seemed to resonate from the walls, the ceilings, and from the bodies of all those present there.

'Comrades, we are at war. Yes, war! The days of our romance with parliamentary democracy are over. The so called Communist Party that formed the coalition government with bourgeois parties with the promise to stand by the peasants and workers, proved that they are hungry for power and for that, they can even co-habit with the bourgeois forces. They expelled the sincere revolutionary leaders like Charu Mozumdar, Kanu Sanyal, Sushitol Roy Chowdhury, Jangal Santhal, and Saroj Dutta from the party. But even then, they could not remain in power. They were thrown out after nine months and now they have again been thrown out after being 13 months in power. Still they are not ready to accept what Comrade Lenin had said—"The Parliament is a pig sty" and that there is no substitute to armed revolution. They are traitors of the communist movement. They betrayed those peasants of Naxalbari, who fought against the landlords for their land, believing that they would get justice from their own government, the United Front, whom they had voted for. It was not only betrayal; it was a genocide of men, women, and children by the combined forces of the police and the *jotdar*s with tacit support from the government of the day. Not only Naxalbari, the bourgeoisie tried to suppress each and every organized movement of workers, wherever it bloomed in the country. Our Polit Bureau member, Comrade Appu from Tamil Nadu, was killed by the goons of *jotdar*s while he was on his way to attend the Central Committee meeting in Kolkata. Your friend, Comrade Chapal Adhikari, has been killed in cold blood inside Midnapur jail along with many others. Thousands of brilliant students of medical colleges, Presidency, Scottish Church, Jadavpur University, and many other institutions dedicated themselves for the cause of revolution. They have fanned out to villages to mobilize revolutionary forces to surround the cities. Now, we have to ask the question to ourselves: What are we doing? Are we fighting along with the struggling millions? Or, by our inaction, are we supporting the reactionaries?

This very moment, when we are talking here in this room, our neighbouring country, China is fighting imperialist America under the leadership of Chairman Mao. Vietnam dealt a mortal blow to the American army; Che Guevara embraced martyrdom in Bolivia. Chairman Mao in his address on 20 May, gave the clarion call to the workers of the world to unite in the fight against imperialist America and its lackeys. Now is the time to strike.

We have organized ourselves under the banner of All India Co-ordination Committee of Communist Revolutionaries. There are detractors, who still advocate for participation in parliamentary democracy. However, Comrade Charu Mazumdar, in his Seventh Document, gave the clarion call to build up an armed partisan revolution and defeat the revisionists. He has given the final shape to this strategy in the party congress held in May 1970. Guerilla units in the villages will eliminate the class enemies and liberate the area. The revolutionary armies will then take over and organize a people's army to make the area secure for the working classes. To wait for building up mass organizations and mass movements is futile because, that will result in revisionism and facilitate opportunism taking its root within the struggle. We are already running late, comrades. You have to decide right now which side you will take. ARMED REVOLUTION OF THE PEASANTS, ZINDABAD!'

The face of the man, who got up after he finished, seemed very familiar to me. I rubbed my eyes in disbelief and looked at him again. He was our KD Sir, Krishnananda Das, our professor who taught poetry. Since he was no mean poet himself, he ended his short speech reciting a poem written by someone unknown to us,

'Both the groups are face to face today;
No one stands in between.
Will you take their side for a favour or two?
Or you prefer to fight for your own right?
Choice is yours, comrade,
Which side will you take?'

Again there was silence. Most of those in the audience got up and turned towards the door. Just then, someone whispered,

'There is some movement outside. Maybe a police patrol. Please remain here in the room, till we ask you to leave.'

Two-three people escorted the leader out of the room into darkness. We waited there with baited breath for some more time, and then left in groups of two or three. The narrow bylane was dark and empty.

I was so scared that every shadow of a tree seemed like policemen waiting for us. Gour da remained silent all through, till we reached Bani Bhavan. I also followed him silently. By the time we reached our mess, I was drenched in sweat.

I was feeling very nervous during the first three periods. I was very curious to know the secrets Gour da had promised to reveal to me, which pushed me towards the Science Block the moment the bell rang for the break. He signalled me to follow him towards the sand dune at the backside of the college. We sat under a lonely cashew tree silently. After a while, he said,

'Don't get confused from what you have heard yesterday. This is not America, neither this is China, nor Vietnam. We belong to an age old system, which is difficult to break. How can you change the mindset nurtured for thousands of years through epics like the *Mahabharata*, the *Ramayana*, and folklores read and recited day in and day out in every household?'

Gour da leaned on the tree and said,

'Amal, my family belongs to the Dhopa community, much lower in the caste ladder. My parents still wash clothes of the well-to-do families of the village. For that, we get a quintal of paddy from each family every year, an arrangement that had been fixed at the time my grandparents had come to this village and had taken up this profession. The paddy we get is not sufficient for even three months for our family of five, but my father will never even think of quitting the profession, because for a Dhopa, washing clothes is not only his duty, but his religious practice too. He does not understand the meanings of words like "exploitation", "class struggle", and "revolution". He believes in his karma, which brought him to this earth as the son of a washerman. He thinks that if he does his duty well in this birth and remains a true devotee of God Almighty, he will be elevated in his next birth.

'It is not my father alone, the Napits, the Bagdis, the Hadis, the Muchis, and the Doms share the same belief. For such people, Lenin, Stalin, and Mao carry no meaning. Armed revolution is not only absurd, it is a sin, a sacrilege for them. Only leaders like Ho Chi Min, Fidel Castro, or Mao can wean the people of that country away from such an age old belief of inaction and ask them to fight till death to wipe out the vice from the face of earth, because they painstakingly built up the momentum over a long period of time and led by example.

'I would ask you to keep your feet grounded, Amal. These leaders are all very good people, but somewhere they have erred in asking the people to discard the inherent belief of majority of the people overnight by citing the examples of alien countries and swearing by the names of Russian or Chinese leaders. This hasty uprising will lead to a catastrophe hitherto unknown to any of us.'

My head was reeling. I could not fully understand what he was saying. But I knew that Gour da was one of the very poor students in our mess, and he kept himself away from politics in a very subtle way. Very rarely, people around us would advise like him to open our eyes and judge things for ourselves. Instead, we were asked to follow their judgments.

I caught hold of his hand and said, 'I shall be cautious Gour da, but I thought you are one of them.'

Gour da smiled and said, 'Of course, I am one of them. I have also been part of a few "actions", but I have seen the futility of it all.

Hemanta Maity is a more cruel and manipulative *jotdar* than his father, Abinash, who was eliminated. Hemanta has filed innumerable cases against the sharecroppers from which they will never be able to come out. He has already evicted a few of them by obtaining court decree. There are many Hemantas and Abinashes around us. Eliminating one only brings another to the centre stage.'

I suddenly remembered a day in Babulpur. Just a year back, the dead body of Balai babu lay in the courtyard and his son, Prankrishno, wailed at the top of his voice, hurling filthy abuses upon CPMs and Naxals. One name, which had slipped out of his mouth only once, was that of Paran, and he was killed within a few weeks. His father would never have gone to that extent. Those who knew Prankrishno well swore upon God that he was happy inside and thanked the murderer, because whoever killed his father did a favour to him. He inherited his father's property long before he expected it. The first thing he did thereafter was to hatch a conspiracy to kill Paran to avenge his humiliation, though he knew fairly well that Paran was not responsible for his father's death. People also suspected his involvement in the rape of Basanti and subsequent suicidal death of her and Bhola, but there was no proof of his complicity. However, everyone knew that Prankrishno never had any qualms about a few murders or rapes just to satisfy his lust and the people were much more afraid of him than his father.

Gour da pulled a biri out of his pocket, puffed it to blow away the dust and then lighted it. After a deep drag, he said,

'A year before your joining us, Animesh occupied the single room on the first floor of the mess. He was a brilliant boy, secured a rank in higher secondary examination from his village school, and was also good looking. It is because of his charisma that all of us came together, rented this building, and started running the Bani Bhavan Mess ourselves. He was our hero; he always stood by us when we were ill or broke. He was the first to come forward and help anyone in need even though he himself was not very well off. One Sunday morning, we were taking bath together; a soap cake slipped out of Gora's hand and fell inside the toilet pot. Gora announced, 'I shall pay Rs 50 to whoever takes it out from the slime.' Animesh flushed the commode once and then put his hand inside to take the soap out without uttering a word. That evening we had a grand feast out of the betting money.

'I still don't understand, to be honest, how a person like him could become so passionate and obsessed with armed revolution, which they termed as "biplab" and went ahead to behead the statues of Ishwarchandra Vidyasagar and Rabindranath Tagore in his school, where he must have celebrated their birthdays numerous times during his student days. He even went on to burn down the school building, the college library and the laboratory, to destroy the bourgeois education system, and finally joined operations to eliminate "class enemies". Sometimes, I feel that he was so innocent and gullible that he became a slave to the slogans that he used to shout day in and day out and started believing in those. He used to put forward his arguments in favour of killing *jotdars* and moneylenders so passionately, that I had no way out but to concede. In the heart of my heart I knew that we are getting isolated from the common people. They remained silent out of fear, which we perceived as their consent. But people never supported the killing to eliminate the class enemy.'

I could not suppress my curiosity anymore and asked, 'Gour da, where is he now?'

Gour da smiled sheepishly and said, 'I don't know. None of us know exactly what happened with him. Last year the police came to our mess at night, pulled him out of his bed, and dragged him to the van waiting on the main road. Afterwards we came to know that he was kept in Midnapur jail hospital with broken ribs and shoulder. He was charge sheeted in three murder cases of Contai subdivision along with other comrades. Then on that fateful day of 16 December last year, he was among the Naxal prisoners of Midnapur jail, who allegedly attacked the prison guards with iron rods and bricks, broke the locks, and tried to flee. The police opened fire to quell the riot like situation in which some prisoners died and many went missing. Animesh was one of those missing prisoners. Months later, when the police allowed relatives to meet the surviving Naxals, it came out that a truck load of dead bodies had been taken away at night and probably dumped in Kansai River, but his parents don't believe he is dead. They firmly believe that Animesh is still alive and will come back someday in the future, after the situation changes.'

When I returned to Bani Bhavan Mess in the evening, a pleasant surprise awaited me. There was an inland letter for me from Sarasati. In her neat handwriting she had written that Hari would be in Contai for the Zonal Committee meeting of the Krishak Sabha. She wanted me to see him after the meeting. Hari had asked about my address in Contai. She has given him my address, but Hari might not be able to find it out. My immediate tasks were to find out the venue of the meeting, seek him out from amongst the delegates present there, and also arrange a suitable time to see him.

# Babu's Emancipation

During lunch break, I followed Sudipta and asked her about the programme when she was about to enter the girls' common room. She was visibly surprised, and at the same time, very curious. I had to answer all her questions: why I was asking this, who the man was, how I knew him, etc. Only after she was satisfied, she told me that the conference was going to be held in the Town Hall the next day. SS would also be there. She also gave me the information that most probably, Hari would stay at night along with the others coming from outside Kanthi in the party commune at Darua. It was used as a night shelter by party workers who fled from their villages to escape the *jotdar*s and the police.

Next day after recess, I went straight to the Town Hall. I asked someone standing outside the hall about the time by which the meeting would be over. He asked me to go inside and find out by myself. I found Hari outside the auditorium wearing a crumpled shirt and yellowish trousers. He was sitting on a tin chair and talking animatedly to someone much younger to him. I pulled one chair behind him and listened.

'Comrade Shisir, we Adivasis don't want any charity from anyone, be it the *jotdars* or the party. Our people joined the party, because we told them that the party is with the peasants, the landless labourers, and the sharecroppers. We will fight for them and we will fight together. Then, why talk about loyalty now? Can we discriminate between a landless labourer loyal to the party and another who is not, while fighting for *benami* or *khas* land confiscated from the big landlords?'

The man in a tightly tucked half shirt, lost his patience perhaps, and said in an admonishing tone to Hari,

'Won't you understand, Comrade Hari, that we had to build our party from the scratch after our government was sacked by the fascist and reactionary forces? It is the conspiracy that was hatched by Tata-Birla. They want to destroy us, and they will do so by using all kinds of enticements, on one hand, and by applying brutal force through the police and their hired goons, on the other. The period of adversity is the time to recognize friends and foes, who will fight with us and who will not. Unless you reward the friends of the party, why should they stick to us? This is perhaps what Comrade Anupam Panda meant when he talked about loyalty to the party.'

Hari scratched his head vigorously and said, 'This strategy will slowly come down to rewarding your friends, relatives, and lastly yourself, in return of your service to the party. Moreover, you may earn the loyalty of one man by rewarding him, but you will alienate ten others, who would have joined us, had we fought for them, even if they do not attend our meetings or join our *michil*.'

The moment he saw me, Hari stopped the conversation abruptly, got up from the chair, and hugged me. With a big smile he said, 'Babu, you have grown up so much in these few months that I could not recognize you. I knew that you would come. Let us go for a cup of tea and *singara* in the stall, and then we will talk.'

I felt embarrassed and asked, 'Will you not be there in the meeting?'

'You know Babu, I am an illiterate Santhal. I don't understand all those complicated things Marx and Lenin said. Let them discuss and decide,' answered Hari. 'I am only interested to know what I have to do. Once I complete the task given to me, I am satisfied. Now, tell me, how is your college? Is there any problem? Then I can talk to Sudhir da. He is a teacher in Kanthi College (another name for Contai College). A very nice man; very simple and affectionate; he loves me a lot.'

I was surprised to hear him taking the name of Sudhir Giri. I had opted for Political Science as my combination subject, and Sudhir babu was the assigned professor to teach us about the Constitution. His calm and quiet demeanor endeared him to students, even though he was a prominent leader of CPM in the subdivision. He contested the Lok Sabha seat of Contai as a CPM candidate and lost by a very small margin to the Congress candidate. It was a coincidence that we met Sudhir babu as he was coming back from the tea stall. The moment he saw Hari, a rare big smile appeared on his face. 'Arré Hari da, how are you? Why didn't you come to me earlier during the day?'

Hari also smiled and said, 'Sudhir da, I thought you must be very busy now, so I didn't disturb you. After all, you have to look after so many people. Here is your new student; from our village. He is very dear to me. Please take care of him.'

Sudhir babu asked me my name, stream, and year; patted me, told me to meet him in college, and left. I asked Hari, 'How do you know him? You have never been to Kanthi before this.'

Hari put his left arm around my shoulder, and as if divulging some secret, whispered in my ears, 'Friendship made in liquor vends and jail lasts for life. We had been in Midnapur Jail for six months together. Those were the heady days; Sukumar da, Sudhir babu, Montu, and many others were there. They discussed, argued, and quarrelled among themselves throughout the day, but only about the movement, about Marx, Lenin, and the strategy to be adopted to unite the workers, fight against the rich landlords, and bring in a better life for the masses. We won the election, but eventually we were hoodwinked by politicians of other parties in league with vested interest and the fascist forces in Delhi.'

I wanted to change the subject with a hidden objective. I asked, 'What is happening in Babulpur? How is everybody doing there?'

Hari smiled, 'The other day I met Naren dada and told him that I shall go to Kanthi. He requested me to meet you, to see how you are doing here. I shall tell him that his son is now grown up. I am happy that you came to meet me.'

I didn't miss the opportunity, and said, 'How could I have not come? I can never forget the love and care you have always given me. And then, Sarasati wrote a letter about your conclave here.'

Hari struck his forehead and exclaimed, 'Oh my god! I have absolutely forgotten the packet she asked me to give you.' He took out a bottle wrapped in a paper from his side bag and handed it over to me, saying, 'She would have killed me had I forgotten,' and then laughed aloud.

I unwrapped the bottle immediately. It was a bottle of achaar made from berry, jaggery, and spices by her Asha mai, which she used to bring so often for me in school. We used to lick it and talk throughout our way back from school. I have been told many times that it was she, who picked berries and got it dried in the sun, mixed the salt and spices for Asha to just put it in boiling jaggery. I used to make fun of that asking why she left the final thing to her aunt and invariably she would ask me not to eat it if I was not convinced.

The meeting was about to come to a close. Hari took both my hands into his and said, 'Babu, my only dream is that my Sarasati will go for higher studies and make a place for herself in this world. But it is difficult for an Adivasi girl to fight it all alone. I can foresee a very difficult time ahead. Vicious attacks will come down upon us in the coming days. I don't know whether I shall survive that. Sarasati is very touchy about her self-respect. She never tells anyone about her problems except me, even if she has to remain hungry for days. The only other person she can freely approach is you. She depends on your advice. She loves and respects you as much as me. Will you help her when I am not there? I know it is difficult for you, but please keep an eye upon her. Hungry dogs prowl upon young girls in every society, particularly when there is no one to protect them. Just let her know that you are there to help her, nothing more.'

I could only press his hand in affirmation; I was overwhelmed when I realized how much confidence he had in me, so as to entrust the responsibility of looking after his dear daughter, Sarasati, to me, even though I am a Diku, an outsider for the Adivasi society, as she is for the Bengali Hindus. He was perhaps reacting to the gradual erosion of values among the Adivasis and the silent resistance coming from the elders to the determined effort of Hari to see to it that Sarasati pursues her studies. Sarasati has mentioned this many times to me in the recent past. She also told me about one incident. One young Adivasi boy from a neighbouring village tried to take her away forcibly from the Sankranti Mela of Sharshanka by putting vermilion on her forehead with the intention of forcing her into the customary living together before marriage. But Sarasati fought back vehemently, and raised such a hue and cry that the boy fled from the scene along with his family and friends. Notwithstanding her total refusal, the village elders expressed their disapproval of the behaviour of Sarasati in no uncertain terms, but could not go any further because Hari stood his ground.

We were absorbed in our own thoughts. Suddenly, we realized that there was a commotion outside the Town Hall gate. A few stones and bricks rained upon the people inside. Some people were shouting—'Vande Mataram', 'Indira Gandhi Zindabad'! People loitering outside rushed towards the main gate of the hall to take shelter. We saw a few young men, waving the tricolour flag of the Congress Party, throwing stones from the adjacent main road. One or two people had already been hit, and seeing that stones were being pelted on hapless people with renewed vigour, Hari suddenly leapt up and ran towards the stone pelters alone, shouting, 'Cowards! Why are you throwing stones? Come on! I shall give you the fight.'

I tried to pull him back, but failed. He was hit by a brick on his forehead. Blood oozed out from there. By the time I caught up with him, he was already outside the gate. One of them pulled out a cycle chain and swung it, which caught me by my chin. Next time, Hari waved his hand, caught it midway, and snatched it away from him.

After that, it was the wizardry of the lone man wielding the chain against the entire group. Caught by surprise, they fled the scene soundly beaten. By that time, his party workers also came out from the community hall. He suffered a bleeding wound on his forehead, a few hits of the iron chain on his shoulders and chest from the encounter with the Yuva Congress workers, but he stood there ram rod straight without taking any support from others. After much persuasion, he put one hand upon my shoulder and agreed to go to the makeshift party office in the conference venue.

Some people escorted both of us to a room behind the Town Hall for first aid. Suddenly, it dawned upon me that the organizers must have been anticipating that something like this could happen and had kept the first-aid kit ready. I had a small cut, which took only a few minutes to be dressed and taped. They had to remove the blood soaked shirt of Hari to dress his wounds. One familiar voice was giving instructions to the man attending to Hari. When I looked up I recognized him instantly. It was none other than Prof. Shantanu Sarkar, my hero from the very first day in college. I could not believe my ears when he asked me, 'Aren't you from the first year?'

When I nodded, he ruffled my hair and said, 'Brave boy!'

A different kind of reception was waiting for me in the college on the next day. The incident had sparked a lot of rumours in the town during the night itself, which got magnified by morning, and further expanded by the time it reached the college. I was sporting a bandaid on my chin like a trophy. There was a small crowd around me. Everyone was asking about the incident in the Town Hall and also about the Adivasi, who fought so valiantly with the famous *mastaans* of the town, Madhu and his gang, that they had to abandon their plan of disrupting the meeting of the Krishak Sabha. They were forced to beat a hasty retreat. Barid asked me whether Hari had a bow and arrows and had performed some kind of black magic; Anil wanted to know how I knew him. I kept mum to all such questions. How would I explain the strange relationship I had with Hari?

However, the climax of the day was the message Sudipta delivered on a chit in the class itself. After the fifth period, she came to my desk, and sitting by my side, whispered, 'SS told me to ask you to come to his residence this evening. Won't you come?'

I was yet to come out of the shock. Somehow I gathered strength and asked, 'Why?'

She suddenly became sombre and said, 'He wants to marry his daughter off to you. He is determined to get you as his son-in-law. Happy? Will you come or not? We can go together from college, have tea at Mouchak, and then go. I want to hear more about that Adivasi leader from you.'

Something inside me stirred up by the word 'that'. I stood up and said, 'I have nothing more to say. I will go there on my own.'

Sudipta remained silent for a while. She took my hand in hers, squeezed them and said, 'Sorry! I won't ask. Let's go now.'

A light perfume took possession of me slowly. I nodded in agreement. When we were crossing the canal, an evil desire possessed me. I asked Sudipta, 'Will you mind if we take the Srirupa cinema route? We can have mutton *ghugni* from Durga Cabin. I am hungry.' Her cryptic answer was, 'Me too'.

The restaurant was famous for family enclosures separated by wooden partitions and a screen in the passage. Since a girl was with me, I boldly entered one and lighted a Charminar before placing the order. I was surprised to see her smiling. It was a shock for me when she picked up the cigarette from my fingers, finished it in a few drags, and crushed it under her shoe.

Sudipta leaned towards me and said, 'I didn't mean any offence when I asked you about the Adivasi comrade.'

By the time the steaming *ghugni* arrived, I was completely bowled out. I told her everything I knew about Hari, and also mentioned Sarasati. She smiled mischievously and said, 'Amal, you need some life lessons, so that you can handle your situation better. I shall teach you that.'

She got up, came to my side, held up my chin, and locked her lips with mine, pushing her tongue into my mouth. I tasted nectar. My hands hugged her waist. I was pulling her closer, when the bearer knocked on the partition of the cabin, and we fell apart.

# The Boy in the Eyes of the Storm

'Dear Brave Peasant Comrades!'

'We, the people of Bohoragora and Chakulia saw with our own eyes the brutal attack launched by the police against us in Suramohi and its adjacent villages. The police and pramilitary encircled the villages one by one. They inhumanly tortured every one, the women, the children, and the old, whoever came their way. They entered the villages, looted the houses of the poor, and burnt many of those down to ashes. They assaulted and raped our mothers and sisters. Old Ajambar Nayak was brutally beaten to death. They razed the huts of poor peasants in Suramohi and turned the village into a graveyard.'

'Despite the atrocities, the people of Suramohi have boldly declared that the only way for the poor to survive is to finish off the enemy through guerilla war. The plough cannot move, if there are ridges in the field. The ridges have to be removed to till the land and sow the seed. The plant of paddy cannot be saved by uprooting only one chomp of weeds, but each one of those. Similarly, we have to uproot all weeds from the society.'

'The brave peasants of Bohoragora, we don't want to live this life of animals. We will live honourably with our heads held high after finishing off the cruel butchers. Raise your voices and say—

Finish the enemies through guerilla actions
Organize armed guerilla forces in all areas
Keep the fire of Naxalbari, Shrikakulam blazing
Communist Party of India (Marxist–Lenisnist) Zindabad
Long live the friend of the poor, Chairman Mao
Bohoragora Regional Organizing Committee'

The first pamphlet was discovered on the wall of Radhakrishna Sahoo's tea stall at the bus stand. Subal Mondol had reached there at about 4 o'clock in the autumn morning to catch the first bus to attend the court case in Midnapur. He was about to knock on the tin door of the shop and ask Radhakrishna to put the sauce pan on the chullah for a cup of tea. Just then, he saw the poster with an alien face of a man in uniform with a cap, printed in red ink on it, pasted on the door. A chill went down his spine. In a trembling voice he called, 'Radhu dada! Radhu dada! Will you come out for a moment?'

Radhakrishna was arranging coal in the oven. He sensed that something was wrong outside. He scattered the pieces of coal on the burning hay quickly, sprinkled a little kerosene, and left it to catch fire on its own. He also stood motionless for a minute once he saw the poster, but he gathered his strength faster and brought the kerosene lamp out. Together they read it aloud, halting after every word two-three times and sat on the bench. Radhakrishna forgot about the chullah or the tea. He could see his own dead body lying in front of his shop, its belly cut from one end to the other. He recalled that a few days back also, a big crowd had gathered in front of his shop even before the sun had come out fully. Someone had brought the news that another big farmer had been eliminated in Nayagram and similar pamphlets had been found on the walls of a few other houses of the village, including the one on the window of the grocery shop of Haru babu. Everybody got one or the other information to share about the activities of Naxals in the neighbouring villages.

Rakhal Jana loved to tell everybody around him the secret of every incident happening in the village and point out indirectly with a wink that the source of his information was 'you know who', meaning thereby that he was privy to many such important and secret information due to his younger brother, Trailokya, the all powerful Chowkidar of Babulpur. How could he let this golden opportunity go? He shouted at the top of his voice,

'Silence! Silence! Listen to me. These Naxals initially came to Debra, Gopiballavpur, and Nayagram from Kolkata; they are educated young men and women, students and teachers, and are big people in their society. They lived in the houses of Santhals, Kodas, Kamars, and Bagdis, and shared food and water in their houses. They looted guns from the rich people and rifles from police stations. One night, they looted nine rifles from Ruposi Kundo Police Station in Midnapur, along with ammunitions and uniforms. Now, they come in police uniform and knock at the doors of *jotdars*, kill them, and take away guns, money, and gold. Within a week, two *jotdars* had been killed in Debra Thana itself. In Gopiballavpur and Shalboni area also many other people have been killed. They have made their base in Jangal

Mahal. They come out for their operation and go back deep inside the jungle after that.'

He then took a pause and added like a soothsayer, 'They used to come to Babulpur occasionally earlier. Maybe someone from among them had killed Heeru and Balai babu. Nothing happened after that. But now they will make this village their centre of activities. So, be ready for that.' Everyone nodded their head in agreement silently and left the scene.

Kanan was sitting on a bench inside the shop quietly. He listened to every single word that was said outside. When the mob thinned out, he also left the shop and straight away came down to our house with Murari, Dasarath, and Suren. Whenever he felt disturbed, he would unburden his worries before Hari. From his appearance it was apparent that he was very much agitated. While Kanan narrated the incident at Radhakrishno's shop, Hari crumbled black tobacco leaves carefully on his palm, and putting those on a sal leaf, he rolled out a *chuta*. He lighted it just after Kanan finished. Hari took a deep drag and handed the *chuta* over to Kanan to shut him up, and then smiling sheepishly, he said,

'Kanu, if you believe in your people you should not worry. Those who put up the posters came from somewhere else. You must have seen only fear in the faces of the people who gathered there. No one was celebrating the killings mentioned in the poster; why? They did not really believe that the liberation promised by the Naxals could be achieved just by killing one individual. For generations they have seen one *jotdar* replacing another.'

Kanan was visibly angry. He said, 'Don't laugh, Hari. Rakhal openly said that after Debra, it is the turn of Babulpur. The police is also keeping a watch. And you know, you are one of the targets of both the police and the Naxals. You are not going out alone in the night from today onwards.'

'Don't worry. Nothing will happen to me.' Hari declared in an assertive manner, very uncharacteristic of him. 'I am a poor, illiterate Adivasi; an outcaste among the educated, smart Diku leaders of my own party. I have great respect for the young revolutionaries, who sacrificed their comfort, career, family, and friends, and came down to the villages to change the social order. My problem with them is that they don't understand us. They are so preoccupied with the Marxian theory of class struggle that they tend to forget that even a poor landless labourer loves his wife, his children. Their first priority at this moment is not revolution; it is survival of the self and the family. You have to prepare him for that. For this small difference of perception, why would they waste their energy on eliminating a small fry like me?'

Kanan kept himself well informed about the political developments in the state, which never bothered Hari. He respected Kanan for that. His knowledge of state politics was limited to the information he gathered from the party leaflets, the headlines of the party newspaper 'Desh Hitoishi', which he could barely read, or from the lectures he attended. He knew the exact direction of the wind blowing in the minds of the people of Babulpur and nearby villages from his close interaction with them in the *handiya* joints or in the Thursday Haat. But when Kanan would start speaking, Hari would listen patiently.

'Haria, don't make fun of them. After parting ways with the CPM three years back, the Naxals formed AICCR. Right from then, these young men from colleges and universities of Kolkata formed their backbone. Red flags fluttered on the top of the school and college buildings, which proudly declared those as free zones. Beleghata, Baranagar, Behala, Jadavpur, Khardah, and Ichapur became strong pockets of Naxals. Many young boys and girls left their homes in the city and fanned into remote villages to live with peasants and workers when their leader coined the slogan, "Go to the villages and build each of them as another Naxalbari." Some of them died in encounters, many others are still languishing in jail; but you must admit that they made the people aware of their inherent strength and instilled fear in the minds of the *jotdars* and the police.'

Hari stopped him midway. 'I do not doubt their revolutionary zeal, their sacrifice. They fought back to back with the peasants against the police and the paramilitary, and took part in killing of *jotdars* and their henchmen. This is the story of Debra and Gopiballavpur uprisings. The armed movement was led by the likes of Asim Chatterjee and Santosh Rana. All of them were bright scholars. They formed armed groups with tribal leaders like Lebachand Tudu, Bhabodev Mondol, and Gunadhar Tudu, attacked the Ruposi Kundo police post, and took away rifles and uniforms. One constable got killed in the firing. Thousands of peasants marched with arms and harvested the crops of big farmers. They killed Kanai Khutia of Shaldohori, Alok Bhuian of Bhuian Basan, and many others in the span of one year.'

Hari was panting due to excitement and was out of breath. Asha came out that very moment as if she had anticipated this and softly massaged his chest, but Hari swept her away with a wave of his right hand. After a while he resumed, 'Kanu, all these things lasted for just two long years, but since then, a lot of water has gone down the Kansai River. Now all the euphoria has evaporated. Hear from me!

Lebachand and Koni Tudu are in jail today. The army is combing entire Debra and Gopiballavpur together with the police. They don't show any mercy to any man or woman among their suspects. Most often, the men are killed and the women raped, till they pass out. People now want respite from the ordeal. Now they don't give shelter to the outsiders. So, most of them have either been caught, killed, or have fled the scene. Santosh, Mihir, Gunadhar Murmu, and other local leaders are hiding in jungles, but any day they will be killed in encounters or turned into living dead and incarcerated in jail. Whatever happens to them is inconsequential to the movement; the fact is that the Naxals are now incapable of repeating Debra anywhere else. I am sure about that. Do not panic just because a poster or two were put up. Believe in your own people.'

'I am not worried about the Naxals alone,' Kanan said. 'The moment you open a newspaper, there are killings, blasts, combing, encounters; a traffic police stabbed on a busy crossing, three headless bodies found floating in the canal. No! Naxals are not responsible for everything that is happening in the country. If I am killed today and one poster is found near my body on which "Naxalbari Zindabad" is written in red ink, even you will say, "Maybe... Who knows..." And Prankrishno will laugh his heart out. This is exactly what happened with the Forward Block leader, Hemanta Basu, just a few months back, in February. Hemanta babu, the veteran leader of Forward Block, a close associate of Netaji, and a leader immensely popular among the people, was killed in broad daylight. His party said that CPM killed him, CPM said that Congress killed him, and the government said that Naxals killed him; and there was a whisper all around that he had become a threat to each of these parties and so he was eliminated. Haria, I am afraid about this situation developing here, in Babulpur; the posters are a precursor to that.'

Sudenly, Hari shouted, 'I don't care, who kills me—the Naxals, the police, or my party men. Innocent people, young workers are being killed by hundreds in the city streets, lanes, bylanes, in villages and towns. No question is being asked. Who is responsible for letting the situation go out of hand? Is it those leaders, who wanted to bring the revolution riding on a mail or express train; or those, who want it at a time convenient to them?

I am a small fry. If a leader of the stature of Comrade Saroj Dutta can be arrested at night from the heart of Kolkata and next morning declared untraceable, then who cares what happens to the non-descript workers like me in a village or a small town. It is better to be killed by my friends in my house, in my village, than to be dragged elsewhere, tortured, and then killed.'

Everybody present there became numb for a minute on hearing such an outburst from Hari. At last, Kanan asked, 'What happened to you, Hari? Why you are so disturbed?'

'Just a few days back, Sukumar da asked me to meet him. Yesterday I reached Midnapur by the first bus in the morning. I was waiting for Sukumar da in the party office. Suddenly, Shovan da entered the room. His bloodshot eyes, disheveled hair, and dirty shirt-pants made him appear like a mad man. He had come straight from Kolkata by the first local train to meet Sukumar da, to tell him something very urgent. Sukumar babu called Sadhan da to his room, where he was taking his breakfast. After an hour, both of them came out. Sukumar da was visibly distraught. When we asked what had happened, he said,

'Shovan has now confirmed that Comrade Saroj Dutta has been killed in a fake encounter. He had heard from reliable sources that none other than the matinee idol of Bangla screen had witnessed the entire incident with his own eyes. He was so terrified and shocked that he left the city, and is in Bombay now.'

Sukumar da went on speaking as if he was speaking to himself. 'I used to call him "Saroj *da*" and he used to address me as "Kumar". We parted ways in 1967. Our party decided to oppose their party vigorously. He used to attack our party in his articles in *Deshabroti*.

Last year, one night, someone knocked at my door. When I opened the door, it was Saroj da in his patent grey long kurta, white pajamas, and a shoulder bag from Shantiniketan. The first thing he asked was: "Kumar, do you have anything to eat in your house? I am hungry."

I told him, "Saroj da, come in and freshen up quickly. We will have dinner together."

Saroj da laughed heartily and said, "Your party will expel you, if this news goes out. And I shall be killed by next evening." After a pause, he added, "We fought for more than a decade together, went to jail, faced inhuman torture, and even bullets. Where did we go wrong, Kumar? Why are we at each other's throats today?"

However, after dinner, he was his old self. He read out a few poems that he had written recently. One of those poems recited by Saroj Dutta is still with me. Sukumar da took out a crumpled sheet of paper from his pocket and read out slowly:

*Ratnakar*

Bloodied feathers fall on calm river
a sky chewed up through chest-smashing calls of parting
Hunter – the Nishadh –

He stands, shameless, stoic, stark in laughter,
Inebriation of non-violence in hand, red eyes,

Bandit Ratnakar awakes
sad questions in eyes, he stays awake, stunned by this sudden pain
two eyes of one swan – hurt to death
– strewn astray by feet
Rishi, speechless in shame,
Vedic mantras make no answer

Golden dreams of fortitude in eyes,
the Hunter has won
From ashes of forgetting rises –
a past, aflame
Vessels of blood burn in brutal wrath,
Rishi burns in hatred of denial

– Today, by the rice-bereft hut, does she still stay awake?
His lover, her breasts are made of skin – does she hold a baby-skeleton
to her?

In peals of laughter, the Dasyu poet,
– he tears those false flags of non-anger apart!
Day of darkness, fulfilled,
to end by the dimly caving shores

We discussed about everything under the sun except politics and then went to sleep. Even before dawn, he woke me up, and said, "Kumar, I am leaving. I don't know whether we will meet again. I am grateful to you for the belly full of rice and fish curry you offered, and a night's sleep. I don't know after how many months, I have had this luxury."'

Sukumar da buried his head in his knees. After a few minutes, he said in a heavy voice, 'He was as prophetic that night as poets usually are. We never met thereafter, but that question still rings in my ears, "What went wrong?"'

Later, Shovan gave us the details he had heard from his sources in Kolkata.

'The police raided the house of Professor Debi Roy at mid-night after they got specific information that Saroj Dutta has taken shelter in that house. They took both the professor and Saroj babu to the police headquarters at Lalbazar, and then separated them for interrogation. The professor was let off that very night. He was told that Saroj babu has also been released, but he could not be traced anywhere since that night.

There is nothing on record about what happened to him thereafter; but in every lane and bylane of Kolkata, a whisper went around. The superstar of Bengali films had gone for his daily walk a bit early that morning to Maidan. It was still dark. Suddenly, from a distance, he saw a black van entering the Maidan, which stopped near the Aryan Club ground. Sensing danger, he immediately took cover behind a thick bush. From there he saw a few men in uniform getting down and a man in kurta-pajama following them. They walked a short distance towards the monument and stopped abruptly. From their gesture, he could guess that the men in uniform asked the man to go away. The man turned back and looked straight in the eyes of the men in uniform. The superstar immediately recognized him. It was the face of the poet, the revolutionary, the leader of young Bengal, who left his home, studies, career—everything he sacrificed just because of the dream he had in his eyes. The man stood his ground for a while. Did the superstar see a faint smile on his lips? He could not believe his own eyes. There was some exchange of words. The man raised his right hand with a clenched fist towards the sky and started walking towards the monument. Even before he could cover 10 or 15 metres the men behind him pulled out their fire arms and shot him from the back. He did not hear the sound, but saw the man slump to ground in slow motion, just like they show it in films. But he heard guffaws of laughter of heavily drunk voices as they moved towards the dead man. He heard filthy abuses and saw them pulling the body by one leg towards the van and threw it inside, like they throw the carcass of a dog or cow into the municipality truck. The shock was too much for the actor to endure. He sunk to his knees and passed out.'

Everybody present there was horrified into silence for a while. Murari broke the silence and said, 'Hari da, are we fools? If such educated people can be killed like pigs, how could we even dream of fighting with them?'

'When our people won the election and formed the government, we took it for granted that the police will take orders from the party in power and support the poor people in their fight for their right of fair wages and share of land,' said Dasarath. 'But now we know that the police are pawns of the system, and they move as the system wants them to. No individual can fight the system and a well trained armed force, and win.'

Hari took Murari's hand in his own and said, 'How many policemen and EFR jawans are there in our state? Thousands... 15 20 30... And, how many landless kisans and *majdurs*? 50–60 lakhs. Can they kill all of us? No! If we come together and march towards them, they will simply run away. If we are 1, 2... 20, or 30, then yes, we can be killed, like they killed hundreds of young men in Kashipur and Baranagar just a few days back. No one raised a finger, not even their parents, brothers and sisters, though they knew what was going to happen. If we don't take lessons from those incidents, the sacrifice of those brother revolutionaries will go in vain.'

Hari's throat choked. He slumped on the mat and could only raise his left hand to signal them to leave him alone. Asha quickly brought a wrapper and put it upon his body gently, leaving no scope for any further conversation.

# The Boy faces Backlash

There was no one in the village to help us. It was not because people suddenly went against the party and its workers; they were afraid that the wrath of the local landlords and the police would come down upon them, if they were seen with us. The police as well as the landlords kept a close watch on every small development around the village and persecuted all those seen around the party office or the known leaders of Babulpur on any small pretext. Every single leader of the Krishak Sabha was identified. They were excluded from all government schemes and even deprived of the meagre ration provided to the people through the panchayat. It was made abundantly clear that all those seen around the Krishak Sabha members would be given the same treatment. As a result, people were afraid that they would also not be allowed to work on daily wage, nor they would get *dadan* of paddy to tide over the lean autumn period.

Hari accepted this U turn in life in his stride and never complained. He walked down 6 km to Narayanpur every morning in the hope of getting some work as a porter in the railway station or in the warehouses of the wholesalers. Hadam was too old to work as a labourer. So he took his spade to the field everyday and worked in the small tract of land owned by him. For an hour or so, he would feebly try to remove the top soil as much as he could in the hope of keeping the field ready for the sowing season. Then, he would dig for edible roots in the bushes, sometimes he found some, but for most of the times, he would return empty-handed. Naturally, that was not enough to ensure two square meals for four hungry stomachs.

Every day Asha mai boiled rice and served it hot with the gruel, little salt and green chilly before I and Sarasati were to leave for school. Sometimes she even managed to roast one brinjal or a potato and served it with green chili and salt. She procured those by fair means or foul; begged for vegetables from neighbours or plucked a few from their gardens in the darkness of night or before dawn. She would divide it between the two of us with a radiant face on those days. We never asked, nor were told what she, Father, or Grandfather ate.

Hari's visit to Narayanpur station for work was no guarantee of getting work. He had to wait along with the others for a call to unload wheat sacks, tins of vegetable oil and mustard oil from rail wagons, and carry those to store them in the warehouse of Marwari wholesalers. However, his political past resurfaced time and again, coming in his way of getting a regular call. He would wait till noon for work. Then, he would go to the party office and while away his time lying down on a mat till evening, before walking back to Babulpur. Sometimes, someone would offer a handful of muri and green chili, but most of the days he returned with an empty stomach. We, brother and sister, would also drink only a glassful of water each on such a night, before huddling together on the mat using one of Ma's torn saris as pillow. Sarasati would ask routinely, 'Don't you get the smell of Ma from the sari?' I nodded and faded away in sleep.

This year, winter was short-lived. By February, it would be hot during the day and slightly chilly in the evening, but there was wide spread attack of chicken pox in the village. Goddess Badham, in the form of a large oval shaped stone that resided alone under the century-old tamarind tree far away from the village, suddenly got her due recognition. She was installed there by the Adivasis after the heart-shaped stone surfaced while digging the ground during the construction of Hopon's house. Sanatan Manjhi, the head priest of Adivasis of Babulpur, grabbed the opportunity with both hands and declared it as the age-old deity of Santhals, who graced them in this alien land to protect them from epidemics like cholera and small pox. He pragmatically used his knowledge of traditional herbs, and freely distributed extracts from plants like *giloy*, neem leaves, and dried *haritaki* fruits along with offerings of fruits and sweets as blessings of the goddess. This concoction, most often, gave relief from excruciating pain to the people infected, but people believed more in the vermilion taken from the body of the stone goddess than the herbs. The stone was as pock marked as the skin of a pox survivor. The face of Sanatan also bore such marks, which proved that he was a survivor. So who else could prevent the epidemic? It was, therefore, no wonder that Sanatan Manjhi, the priest of the goddess for the past many years, shared the seasonal bounty of the devotees.

However, Sanatan explained the phenomenon in a different way. 'Mother Goddess is the woman we always dream of as the cherished one in our own lives; powerful, benevolent, and charismatic, for which people bow before her. She has to be propitiated in the same way we try to please any other woman, by offering cosmetics like vermilion, colourful saris, delicacies like *payas*, *pithe*, fruits, and flowers. In return, she wields her supernatural power to help us in times of distress.'

The epidemic this year came as a boon for us, brother and sister. Sanatan would keep aside a portion of the offerings he got as the share of the priest, Burah Manjhi. On his way back home at night, he routinely knocked at our door and gave us a packet full of offerings. It was a sumptuous feast of *payas*, *pithe*, and fruits, though slightly stale after being kept in the open for a day.

Our anxious wait for Sanatan was not confined to the offerings alone. We knew that we had to somehow bring in a reference to the goddess of Badam Pahar and the old man would forget everything else. He would sit down there and start telling the story how Goddess Badham appeared for the first time, a story he had told us many times before. At that time of night, we would gulp down the offering and listen to the old story once again, narrated by him in his inimitable way:

'On the first full moon night of the spring season, people of our tribe walk down for hours from their villages and assemble around the century-old tamarind tree at the foothill of Badam Pahar under which the stone replica of the Mother Goddess rested. She manifested herself there before Nuju, the Burha Manjhi, and then remained there for posterity in the form of the stone with the imprint of wide eyes and smiling lips. She protected her children from those natural calamities and epidemics, which extinguished the blazing lamp of life in scores across the villages every year.'

We pestered him to tell us the story of how the goddess appeared before Nuju for the first time. Every time he would fold his hands and touch his forehead with closed eyes, as if he was asking for forgiveness from the goddess, before narrating the sacred story of her appearance in human form.

'It all happened hundreds of years ago. An evil spirit in the form of a man descended on earth from the sky. His skin was so white that his blue veins carrying blood were clearly visible; his eyes were brown like a fox, and his hair golden. Young men and women found him so attractive that they clung to him like flies stuck in honey. They sang songs and danced till late night. Women fought with each other to sleep with him at least for once. Perhaps they thought that if they conceived through him, they would be blessed with a child with fair skin and brown eyes like him.

'However, very soon, big bleeding chancres manifested on their groins and genitals. These were very painful and debilitating. None of the traditional medicines worked upon those patients. Slowly, one after another, they died; few others maimed for life. It spread to children faster and the death rate was higher. People started fleeing villages to escape from the killer disease. At last, Nuju, the Burha Manjhi of five villages, as old as the largest sal tree of the village, decided to visit the abode of Marang Buru, the supreme God and Jaher Ayo, the supreme Goddess in the hills of Badam Pahar, surrounded by dense forest and full of ferocious animals like wolves, tigers, and hordes of wild elephants. They walked on empty stomach, even though a feast was spread before them in every village they crossed. Nuju refused to eat even a morsel. His steps wavered, hands trembled; he started sweating, but he administered an oath to his followers that come what may, they would continue the journey, even if he could not. On the full moon night of spring, they reached the foothill of Badam Pahar, distinguished by the red soil under their feet. They decided to halt for the day under the huge tamarind tree. Suddenly, Nuju heard a moaning female voice from within the dark shadows of the trees. He got up with a lot of effort, leaning on his trusted bamboo stick and also picked up a cassock full of water. Everyone around him howled in protest. How could he venture into the darkness of Badam Pahar, the den of evil spirits, at night? But Nuju asked, "What if somebody really needs water? She may survive, if she gets a few drops." Nuju went ahead despite his debility and breathlessness.

'Nuju later described what he saw there. An old lady in tattered clothes, smeared in excreta and pus from the chancres upon her skin, crying in pain and asking for water. Nuju poured water into her mouth, cleaned her face, and washed her body. Then he tried to lift her up on his shoulders to carry her back to their night shelter. She was stone-heavy. Suddenly, the old lady straightened herself up on her own, throwing away Nuju like an insect from her body. She was draped in a red coloured sari and smeared with vermilion all over. She sat erect and laughed wildly. She was very happy, because Nuju was so brave and benevolent. Thus, Goddess Badham revealed her identity to Nuju and asked him to follow her directions to get rid of the disease.

"Isolate the people afflicted with the disease including the alien, and put them up in one hut far away from the village; administer a paste of neem leaves on their bodies and serve them a concoction of bitter herbs as the only diet for a month. Let others shun animal flesh and liquor, and abstain from sex for a month."

'Thereafter, she transformed herself into a stone replica of hers under the great tamarind tree.

'After coming back to his people, Nuju went into a trance and repeated what he had heard from the Goddess. He sternly ordered his companions to follow the measures revealed to him by her.

'The villagers of those five villages obeyed Nuju in letter and spirit and got rid of the deadly disease. However, the alien and most of the people already affected by the deadly disease perished in the quarantine. Grateful villagers came back to her abode on the first full moon of every spring season with offerings. These would be distributed among the ones present. Only the fortunate would take it with devotion. And you know, the stone replica appeared here in Babulpur after years of fervent prayers by the Adivasis. You are among the fortunate ones to wait earnestly for the offerings blessed by her. I am sure you will be the ones to receive her blessings.'

That night also, we were waiting for Sanatan anxiously for our share of the offerings, but when he came, we saw that he was empty-handed and trembling like bamboo leaves. He didn't tell us anything. He could utter only a few words, 'Where is your father? Go and get him right now!' When Father came out with his bowl of rice beer, Sanatan whispered something in his ears and both of them went out, leaving the bowl of rice beer on the verandah. We also didn't touch our food, though we were very hungry.

Father came back along with Sanatan and Kanan supporting two men, severely injured and bleeding, on their shoulders. We recognized one; he was Subhas. The other one was a middle-aged man, with an unkempt stubble, wearing a shirt and pants so dirty that they looked like they had been rolled in mud, with patches of black stains of blood here and there. His condition was worse, because there were deep wounds all over his body. I understood later that he had been injured in a blast. A number of sharp nails from a countrymade bomb had caused multiple injuries all over his body.

Sanatan asked Hari, 'What do we do now? They should be taken to the hospital in Narayanpur immediately, if we want them to be saved.'

Subhas shouted, 'No! Don't do it. For God's sake, let us remain here. The dogs will tear us apart, once they catch hold of us.'

Everyone looked at him with questioning eyes. He narrated the situation in halting whispers, 'No way! Don't take us to the hospital, even if we die. The police and the COBRA force have been hounding us for the last one week, after an encounter in the Hatigeria jungle. Three of our comrades were killed, two were captured alive and thrashed mercilessly. Only God knows whether they are alive till now. We two managed to escape in the cover of darkness. Then they cornered us in Baligeria during a combing operation. We took shelter in the house of Prafulla, one of our active workers. The COBRA force surrounded the house. When they marched in with rifles pointed to the door, it was Prafulla, who pushed us aside, and opened the door. He was gunned down at that very instant, but that gave us time to run away from the house through the back door. The lackeys of the *jotdars* followed our trail, confronted us, and attacked with choppers. Robin dada had been dealt a few blows by the time he could fire. He killed one with his revolver, while I fenced off the blows with whatever I could lay my hands on. They overwhelmed us by sheer number. We had to use the last weapon, few of those very powerful handmade bombs, left with him in his bag. They were thrown out of our trail, but we also got some pellets in our body. We walked during the night, took shelter under the cover of thorny bushes during the day, and lay on empty stomachs, without medication. We ran again at night to cross the Subarnarekha River by hook or by crook, so that we could reach Babulpur. I know we are safe here, even if we have to die because of the rotten wounds. But believe me, that would be much more peaceful than dying a cruel death after having each nail pulled out, skin burnt by cigarette butts, and fingers broken. Don't send us to the hospital, Hari bhai, for God's sake; don't hand us over to them, to die a dog's death.'

No one spoke for a while. Hari broke the silence. Crouching near the semi-conscious man, he observed him for a while, and then asked Subhas, 'Do you know that this man is otherwise also going to die very soon? He is still bleeding. Moreover, how long can we hide him? If they know that you were there at Baligeria and Hatigeria with them and have survived, they will definitely keep a watch for you in Babulpur.'

Sanatan Manjhi could not maintain his equilibrium. He shouted at the top of his voice, 'Then why did you bring them here? Now, the entire village will be ransacked by the bloodhounds, the COBRA forces, trailing traces of their blood. Even after they leave the place, the stench will remain here for many, many more days.'

Hari remained silent for a while, and then, firmly answered, 'They are not going anywhere. Subhas and his friend are our brothers. We may be pursuing different paths, but our goal is the same: a society where a poor Adivasi stands on the same pedestal with a *jamidar* (zamindar) and the son of a labourer gets the same opportunity in school and college to compete with other boys for his place in this world. Take them to the Lodha huts in the outskirts of Kamar Danga. Ask Kanu and Badal to keep them in the underground tunnel that they had dug for storing mahua flower and liquor.'

No one contradicted him; no one said anything in his support. After a minute or so, Kanan lifted the limp body of the man with a stubble on his face, upon his shoulder effortlessly, and went out with Subhas and Sanatan. Hari picked up the bowl and went on sipping the remaining portion of rice beer with his head resting upon his left knee.

We, brother and sister, heard everything from inside the hut. Sarasati whispered in my ears, 'Don't utter a single word to anybody. If the police get a whiff of it, they will kill Subhas kaka and that man. Father will also not be spared.'

When I asked her why they would kill them, what they had done, Sarasati kept mum. She didn't know why, but that was what she had gathered from what Sanatan, Subhas, and even Father said. She was witness to the chain of events that had followed after the battle of Nuapada between the peasants and the goons of the landlord, the day the police had cordoned their hut, Hari was dealt a fatal blow on his head, and his unconscious body had been thrown like dead cattle into the jeep.

The moment I saw the man lying unconscious on the verandah, his swollen lips twitching intermittently, his sprawling hands and legs so thin that they seemed to belong to a teenager, these questions haunted me, 'Who was this man? Why was he here and for what?' It was clear to me even at that age that the man didn't belong with us; he was not even one of the Dikus we normally saw around us. I couldn't forget the face of that lean, thin man with a stubble on his chin, faintly resembling the photos of great leaders that we saw hanging in the party office. Someone told us that these were the photographs of Lenin and Ho Chi Min, leaders, who led their country on the path of revolution and succeeded. I believed that he was one of them, but discovered years later that in reality, he was a well known scholar and lecturer in Jadavpur University. As a teacher he was loved by his students, as a human being he was kind, compassionate, and respected by all those who came into his contact. But he left his family, his job, and came down to live in the villages inside the jungle with poor Adivasis, shared their food and drink, and even followed their rituals. Robin followed his leader and the slogan, 'We will make our base in the villages, form guerilla units, and surround the cities. Our first priority is to eliminate class enemies.'

No doubt enemies were killed; guns and rifles were snatched. The call for the peasants and labourers to confiscate the properties of the rich farmers and distribute those among the landless found a tremendous response from the people, particularly the young ones. They rallied behind their 'Comrade Dada', and many guerilla units were formed with young revolutionaries, who believed that power comes with the barrel of the gun. For the first few months, it looked like Spring Thunder had swept the entire sub-division.

However, it went wrong. The party decided to fast-track the long and arduous journey towards revolution. The emancipation of people in the villages through class struggle was ignored. The emphasis was on the educated middle class in the cities. The leaders, in their hurry to capture power, relentlessly provoked the workers to strike their enemies off. Among those killed, along with landlords were poor labourers, most of them Adivasis and lower caste people, on mere suspicion of being informers or siding with the *jotdars* for getting a few kilos of paddy as *dadan*, teachers allegedly imparting anti-revolution lessons, workers of rival parties, police constables and even poor chowkidars from the village. People were more afraid of them—the revolutionaries, than the police or the paramilitary. The urban revolutionaries no longer remained the fish they earlier used to be, in the big pond. They floated on the surface and gasped for air and became proclaimed offenders, mere criminals. Sensing the opportunity, the empire struck back. The entire police force of the districts, along with the paramilitary forces, descended upon the pockets of rebel stronghold like bloodhounds let loose. Robin and Subhas had to run like two beaten dogs from the territory that they had thought they had liberated, just a month before.

For days and weeks, we didn't hear anything about Robin or Subhas, as if they did not exist anywhere in Babulpur. Then, one evening, someone shouted at our door, 'Hari da!' I opened the door and saw the bearded man in the same shirt-pants, standing awkwardly at our doorstep, leaning towards his right. I routinely said, 'Baba is not well, but wait here. Let me ask him.'

When I informed Father about the visitor and reminded him about that fateful night, he immediately left his bowl of rice beer in a hurry and rushed towards the door. He hugged the man as if he wanted to hide him within himself, and almost carried him inside our hut. They both sat on the mat, where Father kept his pillow and a *kantha*. From his back, I noticed that it was the emaciated body of a man slightly stooping, but when I looked at his face I saw something which is etched in my mind even today. I could never forget those two eyes burning like charcoal from behind the spectacles in that dark room. Father began with an admonishing tone, 'Comrade, you could have asked someone to inform me that you wanted to meet me. I would have come myself. Why did you take the risk of coming out in the open?'

I heard his voice for the first time and I was mesmerized. In a very soft and sombre tone, he said, 'Comrade Hari, this is not the time to sit idle. You know what has happened in Debra and Gopiballavpur. Our fight for land for the peasants was ruthlessly suppressed. We decided to opt for armed resistance against the state forces to survive, and resorted to guerilla action to eliminate class enemies, following the line of action propagated by our supreme leader. We succeeded in mobilizing four thousand peasants and harvested the entire crop of the *jotdars* of three blocks. We snatched their guns and fought pitched battles with the forces but from there things went wrong. We were asked to continue the action against individuals instead of consolidating our gain through political mobilization of people. Consequently, when the police and paramilitary forces stormed village after village and razed everything to the ground, arrested people indiscriminately without any warrant, peasants abandoned the struggle and fled. Our peasant leader, Lebachand Tudu, has been arrested from a hospital in Kharagpur. The party workers now stand isolated from the people. This is our last chance to mobilize the people once again through armed resistance.'

Father had been listening to him patiently till now. He suddenly intervened, 'Comrade Robin, I have also met Lebachand and have talked to him, when he was being treated in a nursing home in Kharagpur, recently. Tell me, where were your other leaders? Most of them have also taken shelter in Kharagpur, though they were physically alright, leaving the peasants to their own fate, while their houses were torched, their women raped. They have lost whatever little they had. What will you do now? You cannot do anything! Comrade, your party betrayed them and lost them forever.'

That was the first time I heard his name loud and clear: 'Robin'. The frail man listened to Father patiently, but his face turned purple. When he looked up, I could see his bloodshot eyes. He said, 'Hari da, I don't know whether we were right or wrong, but I cannot leave my comrades. I want to go back to them as soon as possible, even at the risk of getting caught, tortured, and killed. So many people sacrificed their lives for bringing in the revolution we had promised to them. The martyrs' blood cannot go in vain. I shall carry the red flag, even if I am alone. Do me a last favour! Help me to get out of this place, so that I can go to Kharagpur, and meet our comrades, and then...'

Father got up abruptly and raised his voice for the first time, 'Robin! Tell me the truth! Haven't your people killed Daso, Muni, Surai, and so many other comrades of my party, just because you people wanted to spread your base among those who these peasant leaders brought into the movement under the banner of another party? Who were they? Poor peasants! I don't believe that you are not aware of it, but even then I gave you shelter and helped you to recover from your injuries. Why did you people do it? What I understand is that they were killed because your leader was in a hurry. You didn't have time to convince them to join your party, so you killed them. Now you are asking me for my help to get out of this place to reach your people, so that you can kill some more of my comrades. You have started this fratricidal war. But believe me! We will finish it, not you, because we have the patience to build a people's movement.'

Robin also left the mat, taking help of the bamboo pole of our hut and stood facing my father, looking straight into his eyes. He touched Father's shoulder and said, 'I can understand your feelings, Hari. I had felt the same way when bright young boys of our party were rounded up in Baranagar, Kashipur, and Sinthi, just before Independence Day, by the so called 'Resistance Committee', with the help of the police and paramilitary forces. Most of them were killed in cold blood, loaded in trucks, and their corpses were thrown into River Ganga. And do you know, who led the police and CRPF to their houses and hideouts? The anti-social elements, those who change their colours after the change of every government; but behind them, were cadres of *your* party, who not long ago, were *our* comrades and from whom we separated, just for the sake of our difference on the path the revolution should take.'

He stretched out his arm, caught hold of Hari's right hand, and said, 'Let us forget all this for a moment. I know you have confronted your people and even your party leaders just to protect us from the police. I shall not let you sink into more trouble. We are leaving tomorrow. You have done so much for us that no word is sufficient to express our gratitude. But one word of caution: many of your party men are petty politicians and not revolutionaries. If you believe that they will be by your side during the long struggle in the path of revolution, you are living in a fool's paradise. We may be wrong, but you are being misled into believing that you are destined to succeed. Good bye, comrade! Long live the revolution!'

Every evening we used to turn the pages of our books till kerosene lasted in the lamp. Asha mai cooked rice and whatever vegetable she could manage, in one corner of the hut. When the lamp gasped for kerosene, she served food to us, but she herself would wait for Father to come. That evening, even before we had started eating, Father came back and asked, 'Asha, do you have something in your handi? I have to go somewhere immediately. I may not come back tonight.'

Asha stood still where she was for a minute, and then retraced her steps towards the verandah where Hari was sitting. She looked into his eyes and asked him straight away, 'Where do you want to go at this time of the night? It cannot be a meeting, I know. You should not go anywhere alone. Where is Kanan?'

Hari fumbled, 'No, Asha. Please don't stop me. I have to go. Subhas and his friend are in danger. Our own people have informed the police. They may raid Kol Para any moment. I have to take them out of Babulpur. I, the son of Hadam, the grandson of Matu, had promised them safety in my village. They will have to kill *me*, before they can touch my comrades.'

After gulping down a few morsels of rice in a minute, Hari almost ran out of the hut. But to our surprise, Asha mai also followed him into the darkness without saying a word to us. She came back running. We were stunned when she pulled out a *dao*, a glittering scythe, from the sack of implements lying in a corner of the hut. She again ran out into the dark of night, leaving us in a state of shock. She left her share of the rice gruel untouched in the pot. Sarasati picked it up, put a lid over it, and kept it near the *chullah*, in the hope that she would eat it when she came back.

We came to know about the happenings of that night much later, piecing together the various versions we heard from different people. Father reached Kol Para just in time to take out Subhas and Robin from the dugout of the liquor brewers and ran towards Manoharpur station along the railway track. Within a few minutes, the police and COBRA forces surrounded the huts. Muni and Khudi, two young workers of the party had led them to the hideout. It took several precious minutes for the police to ransack the dugout in search of the fugitives, but they could not get anything except for the torn clothes left by Robin and Subhas. The moment they realized the futility of it, their patience ran out. They pulled down Kanu, Tikam, and Bhutu by their hair and kicked them in their faces, stomachs and groins, till they bled from all their orifices. When they confessed, it was a shock for the police as well as Muni and Khudi.

'Hari took them away from the hut a few minutes before you people arrived.' But no one knew where they had gone.

Sub-Inspector Sunil Bose pushed Kanu inside the jeep, and drove towards south, keeping a close eye on the muddy track looking out for any sign of Subhas, Hari, or Robin. He rightly believed that the three of them would wait near Manoharpur station to board the morning train, if they got the slightest opportunity to sneak in.

After a few minutes' drive, suddenly, Choto Daroga, Sunil babu, spotted some movement inside a bush to his left. He shouted, 'Stop!' and jumped out, even before the jeep slowed down, but when he focused his torch on the bush, there was no sign of anyone. Even the tiny leaves of the bushes hung limp as if in deep sleep. No one else had seen anything. So they wanted to move ahead, but Sunil babu always relied on his hunch. This time he asked the constables also to move further down and search the bushes. He was proved right when they spotted the silhouette of a woman running away and vanishing into the darkness. Sunil babu signalled others to stop wherever they were and ran behind the shadow like a bull that had smelled a cow on heat.

For a few minutes, there was no sound anywhere except the buzz of crickets. Suddenly, there was a shrill cry of a woman followed by a hoarse scream of a man after a few seconds. Constables ran towards the source of the sound, disregarding the sharp pricks of thorny bushes. When they finally located Sunil babu, he was lying in a pool of blood. Apparently, a scythe had sliced through his shoulder and chest. He was holding a torn piece of blood stained sari in his clenched fist. There was no sign of anyone around except trampled shrubs towards north, which could have been a possible trail, but the constables thought it would be wiser to carry the Sub-Inspector back to the jeep, as their first priority was to save his life. They abandoned the search for the Naxals, left Hari's trail, despite his audacity of snatching away a hard core Naxal from the jaws of the police with choicest abuses, 'Son of a bitch! Swine! Where will you escape? You have to come back straight into our net within a few days. Then, we will break your bones one by one.'

We woke up hearing a muffled cry. It was still dark outside. Sarasati rushed out. I followed her. Asha mai lay sprawling on the floor of the verandah taking support of the wall. Her sari was torn to pieces; deep scratches on her breast went down towards her abdomen; her hair was disheveled. Sarasati ran back into the house, brought a *kantha* and covered her bare body. She looked at us like a witch with blood shot eyes, and again broke down, sobbing. Sarasati hugged her, brought her head down upon her little lap and patted her back, as if caressing a small child.

Strangely, Asha calmed down and only long drawn sobs continued. In between the sobs, she whispered: 'That Street dog pounced upon me, Sarasati! ...tore my clothes!... I tried to run away but couldn't... Claws of that wolf skinned my body...it's burning... My whole body is burning, Sarasati! I wanted to kill him...behead him. But I could not.'

While mother and daughter wept together, I kept staring at the two for some time. And then putting my hands around Asha mai, I prayed for my father's early return.

A jeep load of police came in the evening. They dragged my father out of the hut, and handcuffed him before putting him inside the jeep. It was clear that the police had erased the woman from the scene to save Sunil babu from the scandal. A case of attack on the police by Naxal leader, Robin Bhattacharjee, and his partner, Subhas Soren, was filed and Hari was named as an accomplice. The word went around among the local committee leaders that the party would not intervene. Hari had defied the party in trying to save two diehard Naxals. But the case was dismissed within a month after the police submitted before the court that both Subhas and Robin died in an encounter with the police in Jangal Mahal, 100 km from Babulpur.

# Babu returns from Town

I was back in Babulpur for good. There was no reason for me to stay back in Kanthi after the final year examinations. Both Sudhir babu and Shantanu Sarkar, our dear SS, were with us in the dinner hosted by SS in his flat on the last evening of our examinations. SS slapped me on my back patronizingly and said,

'It is now your call. You can stay back in Kanthi and work for the party. In the last few years, you have worked very hard in the student front, with the peasants and the youth. You can continue to work for us, like Biren and Nirmal. You also have the option to quit politics and pursue your studies seriously. I know you will do well there too. But my advice for you will be to go back to your village and work there for the party. I know that your family background will come in your way, but that is the challenge you have to accept, if you want to contribute in the peasants' struggle. It is up to you.'

Everyone looked at me. I looked at Sudipta. But her eyes were fixed at her own feet. From the very first day in college, she had stood by me. Sudipta had taken me to meet SS at his residence for the first time. That was the turning point in my life. I freely used the large collection of books neatly arranged in the racks of each room. She even taught me how to dress. Her strict instruction was to tuck my shirt in for all formal occasions. We talked in English as much as we could to hone our language skills. She was a good listener. Slowly, she extracted from me everything about my past, including my relation with Sarasati. I was in awe of her, for the ease with which she moved around among us, the boys, with supreme confidence. But at this crucial juncture, she didn't help. I could understand that she looked away from me intentionally. So I decided to evade the issue for the present.

She belonged to an educated family of government employees, teachers, and doctors. Her father was an active member of the party in the teachers' front. As soon as she joined Bramho Girls School in Kanthi, she successfully mobilized students under the banner of SFI and formed the students' union for the first time in the history of the oldest girls' school of the district with a conservative Bramho management. But I was sure that she was hiding her worries from all of us. Every time I asked about her family, she smiled and skirted. After dinner, I accompanied her upto the gate of the girls' hostel. She didn't utter a word. Just before she entered the gate, I whispered in her ear, 'Tomorrow we are meeting at my place. I need to talk to you.' She looked at me, but didn't answer.

We reached the college library to return the books almost at the same time. After collecting the clearance, I was waiting outside. She came and signalled me to move on. She joined me at the Canal Road, and together we went to my room in Bani Bhavan. I bolted the door and pulled her closer. Her hands were on my shoulders. We hugged, kissed, and shed tears upon each other's shoulders for a long time. Sudipta disengaged herself and made me sit quietly on the cot. She wiped her face and mine with her handkerchief and sat facing me, on the cane stool. She took some time, perhaps to gather herself, and said,

'I have to go back. Physically, we will be far away from each other. We will never meet again, at least not in the near future. And why should we? You are a fool. You are a misfit in the college, in the students' union, in the party debate, in the conference, everywhere. You have no future, neither in politics, nor in career. The world of politics is a world of make-belief. Anyone can speak for hours on Marx, Lenin, and Mao, without believing a word written by any of them, but he will expect that those who are hearing him, will believe every word, because he said it. You are one person, whom I have never heard uttering even one word that you yourself don't believe. That is why you could become one with those faceless, nameless people. They understood you much better than any of us. I would have loved to be with you and with the people, rather than shouting Marx, Lenin, and Mao at the drop of a hat and fighting among ourselves for power and position. But life on this earth is different from the life on the moon—that is how we have lived like in college.'

I could not resist myself and tried to kiss her. She did not resist, nor did she reciprocate. Her cold dry lips shocked me. She perhaps realized. From the close proximity of my chest, she whispered in my ears, 'As the eldest among three brothers and sisters, I have to take care of my family. Perhaps, you will also be better there in your village with your family and your people, rather than planted here in a pot, blooming like a single rose, big but without any fragrance. So, go back. I shall be happy to carry your memory for life, and happier, if you remember me as the one who loved you for nothing.'

Thus, I decided to leave Kanthi. During the last three years, the Bani Bhavan Mess, the college, Srirupa and Udayan cinema halls, the party office and commune, and above all, my comrades had become a part of my life. I had spent days and nights roaming around the villages in Ramnagar, Satmile, Egra, and Mohanpur with them in summer, winter, and rain. We had starved together. We had also chilled at remote sea beaches, drinking country liquor with a handful of soaked grams mixed with salt, ginger, and chilly, and sometimes with fried prawns brought directly from the net, sitting in the huts of fishermen.

The parting scene was emotional, but did not last long because, except for Biren, others were also going back home. Biren's father was an active worker of the undivided Communist Party. He went missing one night and never came back. The rumor was that he had been kidnapped and killed to uproot the nascent peasant movement from his village. His mother also died within a few months. Sudhir babu, our professor, got him admitted in the college and accommodated him with his family.

A lot had changed during the last three years in Babulpur. My grandfather, the head of my family and the mukhia of the village, was terminally ill. Asthma ate up his stamina so much that he gasped for his each breath. Only the bony cage of his ribs heaved every time he drew air, lying curled up on one side of the huge wooden bed, which we had nicknamed Mayur Palank for the two peacocks carved on the black teak wood at the head and the foot. Within a few days, I discovered that the old man had lost his will to live, after he had to surrender to the government acres of farm land that he had acquired so painstakingly, due to the land sealing fixed for each family. Our family could retain only about one third of the total land. Grandfather was so hurt that he stopped speaking even to my grandmother and gradually confined himself to his bed.

The meeting point of the people of Babulpur and the nearby villages shifted from the affluent houses of farmers to the makeshift bazar mushroomed in the junction, where one road coming from the east, from Nuapada, and the other from Lajpur, met the metal road. It became the recognized bus stand for surrounding villages. People flocked to the lone tea shop since 4:30 in the morning, when the first bus would leave for Midnapur. The rich men's luxury of having tea with an elaborate ceremony in fine ceramic cups and saucers was usurped by Radhakrishna Sahoo, a middle-aged man, Teli by caste. He had worked in a tea shop in Midnapur and hit upon the idea to open one in Babulpur. His simple recipe was to boil the water, milk, sugar, and tea together, add pods of crushed ginger in a saucepan, strain it in an aluminum mug, and serve it in small glasses for 20 paisa each. He added *alur chop* and *muri* in his menu soon thereafter. Overcoming the initial inhibition of drinking tea prepared by a Teli, many a Bhadralok like Akhil babu, the post master, Boren babu, the second teacher of the primary school, became regular visitors of Radhakrishna Sahoo's tea stall.

That was where I met Hari one evening. The moment he saw me, he got up and took me in his arms, but immediately he disengaged himself. He didn't say anything to me there, except for the customary: 'When did you come back? How were your examinations?' Before leaving, he whispered in my ears, 'Meet me in the evening at my place. We need to talk.'

When I reached his hut in the evening, he was sitting on a mat in his verandah wearing a worn out khaki shirt and a pair of shorts, most probably gifted to him by somebody, and drinking *handiya*. I settled on the next cot. After a while, he asked me, 'Babu, would you like to have a little *handiya* or a glass of mahua that Supai has brewed himself? My friend from Jokha gifts me a bottle of the first cut, whenever he brews a big pot.'

I must have betrayed my desperation for a glass of liquor with my greedy eyes. Hari read it on my face, and laughed at the top of his voice, as only he could. Touching my chin, he said, 'My Babu is no longer a kid. He has grown up. We offer *handiya* to Marang Buru and then serve it as his blessings to all, even to our children. You can take it as an offering if you like, or you can take it as a drink. Those who drink *handiya* with us even once are accepted as one of our community.'

During the last three years in Kanthi, I had taken to smoking and drinking. We had got used to biri, cigarette, and liquor in the Bani Bhavan Mess. It was the symbol of adulthood. Sharing a cigarette or a glass of liquor was the quickest way of generating trust and friendship among classmates and even seniors in the college. People in the villages invaribly offered *muri* and biri, whenever we visited their houses. A sense of belonging grew when we shared these little things they offered. After I left Kanthi, I no longer enjoyed the regular monthly allowance, nor a little extra income from tutions. Here I had no option, but to buy a bundle of biris with the little money I saved. I didn't have the money to buy liquor. The offer made by Hari kaka now tempted me to grab the bottle and finish it in one go, but I controlled myself. I sensed that Sarasati must be somewhere inside the hut, watching me. So I said in a feeble voice, 'No, Hari kaka, not today.'

I had guessed rightly. She was following our conversation from inside. She came out from the hut and softly said, 'Baba, he is a rich man's son. He is not used to drinking these cheap liquors we Santhals drink. Don't insist. He does not want to drink with us. Fair enough. Why insist?'

Her lips quivered with a hidden smile. She was wearing a sari. In the fluid darkness of the twilight, my eyes got stuck upon the unbridled breast casually covered with the thin texture of the drape. It took me a while to decide. I picked up the pot of *handiya*, gulped down a quarter of it and wiped my face with the lower end of the kurta I was wearing. When I looked up, I saw that Hari was looking away from me, trying to hide his smile. Sarasati sat on the left side of Hari, leaning upon him. Now she took a sip from the same pot. Looking at me from the corner of her eyes, she said, 'Baba, tell him to be very careful. Everybody is keeping a watch on him including the police. If he is found involved in any mischief like last time, he would be straightaway sent to jail.'

Suddenly, the grin vanished from Hari's face. In a serious tone, he said, 'Babu, I asked you to come to my place, because I wanted to discuss something which could not have been discussed outside. Sukumar da came to Babulpur a few days back, and sat here on the same cot you are sitting today. He is now trying to rebuild the party from scratch. He has asked me to give him the names of people whom he can trust. I know how much work you have done for the party in Kanthi. I am very proud of my Babu. I have told him that you will be an asset to the party, not only in Babulpur, but also in the entire Narayanpur Local Committee, or even in the district.'

The question I asked sounded foolish even to me, but I could not control myself. 'Hari kaka, where is the party here? Everything looks decimated. A party needs people as its base, upon which, the structure stands. You people sacrificed everything for the cause of the peasants and *majdurs*. While the party was in power, thousands joined the rally, marched in procession. After the fall of the United Front government, when you became the target of the landlords and the police, your own people remained silent. What are you going to do in this situation?'

Hari suddenly got agitated and said, 'People are people and that is why they are not communists. They are free to be silent or active whenever they choose to, but a communist cannot. He has taken the vow of bringing in revolution: equality in society, freedom from hunger, and land for the peasant.'

Hari was panting. His lungs affected with tuberculosis could not withstand the emotional outburst.

'You know, Babu, I have heard it from my father and grandfather that our Sarna faith forbids taking even a leaf more from the tree than required. It is something higher than what even communism preaches. We believe that Mother Nature is the greatest practitioner of equality, and the most ideal example of what a true communist should be. She only gives; she doesn't want anything in return. Communism is ingrained in our Sarna faith. I want to be a true follower of my faith. And that's why I am fighting for my dream world, which is much similar to the one in a communist country. One thing I must tell you Babu, it is not the party, but a dream, which people follow.'

I felt the rice liquor slowly but surely overpowering me. I could not control myself. I thumped the cot and said, 'You are absolutely right. The history of our nation's freedom struggle teaches us that Gandhiji's dream of freedom through ahimsa got wide acceptance throughout India, but Netaji's call for an armed struggle to snatch freedom from the British had only a few takers, because Gandhiji was able to connect with people even on the street, which Netaji could not. Gandhi was a leader of the masses, but Bose was confined to the educated. In the recent past, people's perception about Nehru was that he is more a saheb than one of their own, but they accepted his daughter, Indira, as their leader, because she convinced them that bank nationalization was a far more socialist step than the rhetoric of communists; she captured the imagination of the people by going to war with Pakistan to liberate Bangladesh.'

Hari took it up from there, 'Go to the people, explain to them your dream, and identify those, who are ready to follow the same. Together with them, you go ahead in the pursuit of your goal. But remember the party is only an instrument. When the instrument becomes bigger than the dream, the followers of the party become a part of that instrument and try to crush whatever comes in its way.'

I attended the party lectures given by highly educated leaders, political scientists interpreting Marx and Engels eloquently. The concept of dictatorship of the proletariat is fine. But when it comes to choose the path to achieve it, everything looks hazy. Hari's words rang in my ears loud and clear: 'Be certain about your dream, be clear about what you want to achieve, and then choose your path. There is no shortcut to life's goal.'

I got up and said, 'Hari kaka, I shall definitely come and meet Comrade Sukumar. Please inform me whenever you get to know the date, time, and place. But I won't commit whether I would continue to work for the party in Babulpur. You know my situation, but there are other reasons also. I am getting disillusioned about the dream I have pursued for the last few years. As you said, the dream is the most important thing in one's life. Please don't misunderstand me.'

When I left him, he was intently looking at the pot of *handiya* and brooding on something, which I could not decipher. All of a sudden I saw him holding the entire pot with both hands and drinking it in one go. Throwing the pot away, he stretched out on the cot.

Unlike him, I felt my head reeling and legs tottering. I knew the reason. I had gulped the thick liquid too quickly. It is supposed to be savoured slowly, and only then it cools the body like the gentle evening breeze that sucks the day's long heat from the trees within no time. But for making any attempt to mess up with the sacred drink, one is punished instantly.

Just after I crossed the stack of straw in the courtyard, I felt a hand on my shoulder. I looked back in anticipation and for the first time, I was proved right. Sarasati was there, leaning back on the stack, and smiling mischievously. Even in the twilight I could see a pinkish hue in her eyes. She said sheepishly, 'Are you angry with me, Babu?' I took a step forward, placed my outstretched hands on her shoulder, and pulled her towards me. She did not resist. She was about to say something, but I sealed her lips with mine. In a flash I remembered the dry cold lips of Sudipta. Effortlessly, I brushed that memory aside. She was right. I belonged to this village of mine, Babulpur. The towns and cities were alien lands for me. Here was my love, in these eyes.

We hugged each other with all our might, as if life was coming to an end in a moment. I removed the sari from over her chest and rubbed my lips all over. She clenched her fist upon my back; her nails scratched my skin and it started burning. We tumbled down upon the loosely strewn hay and started discovering our own bodies, unkown to us until now. A strong aroma emanating from the soil drenched in the first rain filled the air all around.

I came back to my senses after Sarasati gently pushed me away and gathered her sari to cover herself up. We were totally drained out, physically and emotionally. We remained there entangled for a long time. We sat up together, as if on cue. I could not look at her in the eyes, and sat there with my head buried in my knees. It was she who broke the silence. 'Don't get upset Babu; at least, not for what you have done right now. I approached you. You couldn't have touched me without my consent. You don't have to feel guilty, nor solely responsible for anything. I am equally responsible for whatever happened. From the day you came back, I wanted to be with you, because, in your absence I realized that I love you. You don't have to love me back. Socially, we are poles apart, and it will remain so even if you want it to be different. Now, get up and go back home. It is getting too late.'

I was still dazed, as if fire crackers were exploding in my head and spreading out sparkles all around. I could see snap shots of my past reeling out before me. A long procession of people waving flags marched towards the horizon. Known and unknown faces curled up like smoke in the sky. I looked at Sarasati, wondering if she could recognize her ancestors among them. Some of them definitely resembled mine.

Sarasati was the first to get up. She pulled me up by my hands, wiped the sweat out of my face and neck with her sari, patted my shirt to get rid of the straws, and led me out on the road up to the Babui Bridge. I could see her standing there, till I took a turn towards Babulpur on the other side of the river.

# Epilogue

Master was lying on the thin mattress spread over the metallic cot in the isolated corner room of the hospital. Around him were people sitting on stools with all ears turned towards him to catch every single sound coming out of his mouth. He had been administered the serum for the narcotic test. They believed that this frail man was the mastermind of the fire that had engulfed the country during the last five years. He gasped for breath till multiple ampoules were pushed into his vein. His breathing slowed down. With eyes half open, he recited his favourite poem (*The Long March*) in whispers:

The Red Army fears not the trials of the Long March,
Holding light ten thousand crags and torrents.
The Five Ridges wind like gentle ripples
And the majestic Wumeng roll by, globules of clay.
Warm the steep cliffs lapped by the waters of Golden Sand,
Cold the iron chains spanning the Tatu River.
Minshan's thousand li of snow joyously crossed,
The three Armies march on, each face glowing.

Master saw himself standing on the bank of Teesta and reciting this poem written by his idol, Mao Ze Dong, 30 years back. He could see the red flag fluttering in three directions—Andhra and Odissa in the south, Bihar and Uttar Pradesh in the north, and Madhya Pradesh in the west—three armies crossing the mighty river. Men in uniform, armed with rifles, stood on the opposite bank. The war cry of the peasants of Naxalbari, Fansideoa, and workers of the tea gardens, armed with bows and arrows, spears and swords, rose to a crescendo. Volleys of bullets were fired, shrill cries of the people dying filled his ears, and smoke choked him.

He woke up drenched in sweat and found himself on his own bed. His doctor had asked him to avoid exerting himself mentally and physically, if he wanted to live for another few years. But how could he let the golden moment pass by? He had read every line written by Mao over and over again. Chairman Mao had unequivocally said, 'It is only by the power of the gun that the working class and labouring masses can defeat the armed bourgeoisie and the landlords.' Revolution was in the air! It was just the question of igniting the wick. Combat Units were to be formed without any further delay. Annihilation of class enemies, snatching their weapons needed to be started immediately, both in cities and villages. He lifted himself up with great effort. Then he picked up paper and pen, and started writing letters to his trusted comrades: Kanu, Jangal, Khokan, Kadam, and others.

The message spread like wild fire. The first arrow was shot on 25 May, just three months after the United Front came to power in Barajharu village of Naxalbari. While the house of a landlord was being seized, a police patrol entered the scene. Thousands of agitated peasants and workers from tea gardens confronted the police. Three arrows pierced Sonam Wangdi, the Inspector. He died the next day. All hell broke loose. The paramilitary force opened fire upon a women's meeting in the Prasadi Jote of Naxalbari police station. 11 people died, among whom, were 7 women and 2 children. The Communist Movement in India took an irreversible turn towards ultra left. Ajit Pandey sang a song in the street corners which resonated in the hearts of the people of entire Bengal:

*Terai kande go*
*Kande amar hiya*
*Naxalbari maa kande*
*Saptakanya laiga.*
[The whole Terai weeps
My heart also weeps
Motherland Naxalbari weeps
For her seven martyred daughters.]

However, the *michil* of death continued in Naxalbari in front of his eyes. In the open street of Naxalbari Bazar, old kisan Barka Manjhi was beaten to death by the henchmen engaged by the rich farmers. Shovan Ali and Tribeni Kanu died in the police action. Jangal Santhal and thousand other activists were rounded up. He could see the deserted huts and muddy roads; naked children loitering around like destitutes. For almost six months, the entire Naxalbari district remained a battleground between the peasants and the state forces, but these were small sacrifices required for ushering in a revolution. It happened in Russia, China, and Vietnam. It happens wherever peasants and workers take up the fight to establish the dictatorship of the proletariat.

He remembered the huge public rally that had taken place on 11 November 1967 in Kolkata. Red flags converged in Maidan from all directions. Battalions of police lathi charged the peaceful processions to disperse them. Like waves, the mob swept them away. People gave him, a sick man, the strength to pay his tribute to the martyrs of Naxalbari. The enthusiasm of the masses gave them the strength to reiterate their resolution:

'There is no other way. The path shown by Lenin, the way forward taken by Stalin, and the torch kept aflame by Chairman Mao has been reignited in Naxalbari. This is the path of the people of India.

But what happened then? About a hundred battle hardened revolutionary peasants of Naxalbari, led by dedicated comrades, like Kanu Sanyal and Khokan Majumdar, left for the jungles to prepare the base for future guerilla attacks on the police and landlords. It was expected that this guerilla force will multiply with each successful operation. But no one had anticipated that the coordinated attack by the state forces would break the backbone of the peasants; the constant surveillance placed on them would cut off the supply route of food and essentials to the guerilla fighters in the jungles. Many of them fell ill. No food, no medicine, not even potable water was available. The entire unit got demoralized to such an extent that they left the jungle in search of food and fell easy prey to the waiting policemen. Some of them vanished from the face of the earth; most of the others were incarcerated without trial, and eventually shifted to jails in distant lands.'

Did he believe that merely a hundred untrained guerilla fighters could sustain a revolution? No. However, he believed that they would show the path of socialism to millions of others throughout the country, and within a short period, the proletariat of India would rise in rebellion. But essentially, there was too little time. Every breath tested the breaking point of his ribs. Every bout of cough tore yet another vein in his chest. How long? For how long did he have to endure this dreadful existence? Or, was he destined to leave this world, while the people of the country would still be in fetters?

One of those people that Master was worried about was lying on a tattered *madur* on the verandah of his hut in Babulpur. Hadam could barely open his eyes. Through the slit of his eyelids he peeped and saw only eyes all around him, with each pair focused on him. He could not see the faces, but the star studded sky behind them was as luminous as the one he remembered from his childhood. The swan adorned the eastern skyline as usual. All the *hansda*s returned to the abode of swans after death, he recollected. A smile appeared across his wrinkled cheeks just by the thought that Matu, Kapu, Rajo, and Joba—all would be there, along with his long forgotten ancestors, waiting for him to join them.

However, his smile soon faded away. Black shadows engulfed the eastern sky. The face of Subhas came out from the smoke like cloud. Hadam remembered that he was another *hansda*. He looked exactly like the body brought back, wrapped in a gunny bag after post mortem. His hair was stuck all over his face with dried blood. The hole in the place of his right eye socket robbed from his face the vivacity, which was so natural to him. He must have looked as vicious when he was fighting the forces shoulder to shoulder with his comrades. He fell in the encounter after a hand to hand combat; he was shot from point blank range. Subhas was not alone though. There were other faces around him, lurking behind in the background, with wounds on the forehead, the cheeks, and the temple. There were women draped in blood stained pieces of cloth, with deep gushes all over their bodies. They must be *hansda*s from somewhere else, because they were allowed to enter into the territory of the eastern sky. Shadows of these young men and women covered the sky; even the mountain, Badam Pahar, in the background vanished from his mind's eye.

The visuals floating before his mind's eye got mixed up. Though he was a small child then, he could still remember the body of Matu lying in the field along with two other Mahalis, who attacked him at the behest of a *jotdar*. The last time he had seen Rajo—his mangled body on the railway track, he had noticed the silver white cross tied to a black string around his neck. His own people had excommunicated him from the clan just because of that. And he ended his life, leaving Joba and Sarasati to their fate.

Hadam closed his weary eyes. But how could he drive away those voices that kept on ringing in his ears?

'After a tiger tastes human blood, it has to be killed. Or else it will go on killing people at the slightest opportunity. You cannot plough the field, if there are ridges. Won't you remove those, before you take the plough to the field? The crop cannot be saved by removing one clump of weed. Every single weed is to be uprooted. Master has issued clear directions to eliminate the *jotdars* and their cronies to liberate the village from their stranglehold. All other parties and the leaders talk about becoming MLAs and ministers. If we all follow Master's directions, the entire country will become free from exploitation within a year or two.'

Hadam was lying unconscious on a *kantha* in one corner of the hut. Asha had placed a few folded saris under his head. Every few minutes she closely looked at his face. She tried to listen to the sound coming out from his quivering lips, but she did not realize that Hadam was weeping bitterly for Subhas Soren, Shovan Ali, Barka Manjhi, Chapal, and many others. They never cared to learn lessons from the past. Since his childhood, he had heard the stories of many uprisings. From Titumeer to Sidhu-Kanu, there was no dearth of commitment, no flaw in their cause, no chink in their bravery. People rallied behind them and marched ahead to embrace death. They lacked only one thing: the patience of a white ant, the perseverance to build up a sturdy ant hill by silently working for years, which even a bear cannot breach. But what they had built instead was a bamboo fortress, a paradigm made up of a romantic view of the world around. The uprising perished in the gallows, where they were hanged along with hundreds of others. And now, after a hundred years, history was repeating itself; Sidhus and Kanus were being hunted down like wild boors or rogue elephants.

Hadam again looked up at the sky. The faces looked brighter. He didn't know why. He longed to go there to join them and ask them, 'Is the world any better now, after so much bloodshed?' Where was he going to leave his grandchild, the successor of Matu? Was it going to be in the same cauldron of poverty, disease, hunger, and death?

Hadam took a deep breath and consumed the last drop of vitality to get up. His body trembled. A drop of tear rolled down his cheek. His question remained unanswered.

Master opened his eyes. The effect of the narcotic faded. He could see a number of stern faces closing in. Frustration and impotent rage oozed out from their eyes. Someone hissed in his ears like a cobra: 'Speak out! Whom are you trying to shield? Every single comrade of yours has been accounted for. Some of them are in jail and some have vanished. You are finished. Come out with the truth!'

'Truth!' He was feeling suffocated. His face became tense again, the crease upon the forehead reappeared. With it came back the spasms. Everyone stood up. People around him panicked. An oxygen mask was placed on his face, injections were pushed. Amidst all this, his frail right hand went up, with the index finger pointing towards the sky. Before anyone could react, it slowly came down on its own. His chest gave up the fight and his face became serene again.

# Acknowledgements

There are broadly two types of data available on the Naxalbari Movement in Bengal: one, the documents written by protagonists themselves or their adversaries, who looked at the movement from a particular angle, and the other, the written works of political analysts who recorded the chronology of events with a commentary there on. Very little material is available on the inside story of the individuals, who fought the battle in the streets, in the jungles, and perished. I am indebted to those faceless people, who survived to share the anecdotes that I have pieced together while writing this novel.

However, there is much more to this. I have tried to highlight the undercurrents in the minds of the people, which belied the prediction of many political pandits of that period, and simultaneously, I have tried to relate those to the events as faithfully as possible. For that, I have referred to mainly two books, namely, *Naxalbari Ekti Mulyayan* by Suniti Kumar Ghosh, and *Revolution Unleashed* by Amar Bhattacharya. *Rajnitir Ek Jibon* by Santosh Rana, *Collected Writings of Charu Mazumdar*, and *The Naxalites through the Police Eyes* have served as the source of many quotes and anecdotes. The poem, 'Ratnakar', by Saroj Dutta was originally published in Bengali in the magazine *Chatushkone*, in 1992; the present English translation has been taken from the online sources: milansagar.com and aisa.in.

I am grateful to Nirmal Kanti Bhattacharjee for his invaluable guidance in conceptualizing the book, and collecting the source material. I am also grateful to Anindita Kargupta, who played the role of devil's advocate to sharpen the edges. My thanks to my editor, Arunima Ghosh, who spent long hours to bring some sanity to my emotional outpourings.

## About the Author

Born in 1955 in Ranisarai, West Midnapur, West Bengal, Amar Mudi has a master's degree in Mass Communication. The author of the critically acclaimed novel, *Curse of Badam Pahar: Savages of the East*, he has many translation works into Bengali to his credit—Orhan Pamuk's novel, *My Name is Red*, Ismail Kadare's The Successor, Imre Kertesz's *Fatelessness*, and Manohar Shyam Joshi's Hindi novel, *Kyaap*. He has also published a compilation of poems, *Jiban Jatra*, and plays like *Uttaradhikar* and *Thakurdar Coffin*.

**Reviews of *Curse of Badam Pahar: Savages of the East* by the same author**

*A fascinating mix of fact and fiction, history and politics, it relates the story of three generations of a tribal family and its interaction with the 'civilized' world.*

—**Nilima Sinha**, The Book Review Literary Trust

*'Curse of…' is a book which has what can be called political writing as it narrates the challenges and hardships faced by the Adivasis or 'savages' (as the world calls them) in the backdrop of the most crucial movement post-Independence, in the Indian political scenario—Communism.*

—**Ritika Handoo**, Zee News